The Yellow Rose

The Yellow Rose

MAURUS JÓKAI

Translated by

BEATRICE DANFORD

ÆGYPAN PRESS

1896

From the edition published by Jarrold & Sons of London.

Special thanks to Steven desJardins and the Online Distributed Proofreading Team (which can be found at http://www.pgdp.net).

Transliterating the name of the author of this book is a matter of contention: in some volumes it's Mór Jókai. In others, Maurus Jókai or Mor Jokai. They're all the same man.

The Yellow Rose
A publication of
ÆGYPAN PRESS

www.aegypan.com

Chapter I

This happened when no train crossed the Hortobágy, when throughout the Alföld there was not a railway, and the water of the Hortobágy had not been regulated. The two-wheeled mill clattered gaily in the little river, and the otter lived happily among the reeds.

At the first streak of dawn, a horseman came riding across the flat Zám puszta, which lies on the far side of the Hortobágy River (taking Debreczin as the center of the world). Whence did he come? Whither was he going? Impossible to guess. The puszta has no pathway, grass grows over hoof-print and cart track. Up to the endless horizon there is nothing but grass, not a tree, a well pole, or a hut to break the majestic green plain. The horse went its way instinctively. Its rider dozing, nodded in the saddle, first on one side, then the other, but never let slip his foot from the stirrup.

He was evidently a cowherd, for his shirt sleeves were tight at the wrists – wide sleeves would be in the way among horned beasts. His waistcoat was blue, his jacket, with its rows of buttons, black, and so was his cloak, worked in silken flowers, and hanging loosely strapped over his shoulder. The slackly gathered reins were held in the left hand, while from the right wrist dangled a thick stock whip. A long loaded cudgel was fastened to the horn of the saddle in front. In the wide upturned brim of his hat he wore a single yellow rose. Once or twice the horse tossed its head, and shaking the fringed saddle cloth, woke the rider for an instant. His first movement was to his cap, to feel whether the rose was there, or if perchance it had dropped out. Then removing the cap, he smelt the flower with keen enjoyment (although it had no rose's scent), and replacing it well to one side, threw back his head as if he hoped, in that way, to catch sight of the rose. Presently (and very probably to keep himself awake) he began humming his favorite song:

"If only the inn were not so near,
If only I did not find such cheer
In golden quart and copper gill,
I would not linger, my love, until
It ever should grow so late."

But soon his head fell forward again, and he went on nodding, till all at once, with a frightened start, he saw that the yellow rose was gone!

Turning his horse he commenced searching for the flower amid that sea of grass, and the yellow blossoms of cinquefoil, and stitchwort, and water-lilies. At last he found it, stuck it in his hat, and continued his song:

"An apple tree stands in my garden small,
The blossoms it bears they hide it all.
Oh there where the full carnation blows,
And a maiden's heart with a true love glows
Is the place where I would be."

And then he went to sleep again, lost the rose, and once more turned to look for it. When found this time, nestling among a cluster of pink thistle-heads, he nearly kicked the plant to pieces. Because – because it had dared to kiss his rose! Then he sprang back to the saddle. Now had this cowboy been superstitious he would not have decorated his hat for the third time with the yellow rose. Had he understood bird language, he would have known what the hundreds of little larks were twittering as they rose up out of sight, to greet the dawn. "Wear not – wear not your yellow rose!" But this Hortobágy peasant was hard-headed; he knew neither fear nor superstition.

He had wasted a good deal of time, however, in seeking this rose – though possibly more in winning it – for at the watering-hour he should have reached the Zám herd. By this time the overseer must be cursing him roundly. Well, let him curse! When one has a yellow rose in one's cap one is not afraid of an overseer!

The sudden neighing of his horse roused him. A horseman was approaching, whose steed, a bay with a white star, was evidently an old friend of its own. The rider was a "csikós," or horseherd, as could be seen by his wide flying sleeves, white cloak, tulip embroidered, the lasso thrown around his shoulders, and best of all, by the way he had saddled his bay – without a girth. The two herdsmen recognized one another, as well as their horses, and quickening their trot drew close together. Both men, though distinctly different, were of the true Hungarian type, such as were the first Hungarians who wandered in from Asia. The cowherd was broad-shouldered, thickset, and bony, his face roundish and his cheeks red, while there was something of impudence in the chin, mouth, eyebrows, and little waxed moustache. His chestnut hair was cropped short, and his eyes hazel, though at first sight seeming almost green.

The other, the csikós, was strong and square-chested, yet withal slightly built. He had an oval face, burned to a golden bronze, with perfectly regular clear-cut features, eyes dark and shining, and a black moustache that turned up of itself. Over his shoulders his jet black hair fell in loose wavy ringlets.

The two horses snorted in friendly fashion, and the csikós was the first to hail his friend.

"Good day, comrade! You are up early. But maybe you have not slept at all?"

"Thanks. That's true. There was someone to send me asleep and to wake me up!"

"And where are you from now?"

"Only from the Mata puszta. I was at the vet's."

"At the vet's? Better kill your horse at once."

"Why?"

"Than let the doctor and his old nag overtake it. He went by in his gig half an hour ago, jogging along towards the Mata herd."

"Well, well, comrade! The shepherd's white donkey has often beaten your little bay mare."

"Hm'm. What a pretty yellow rose you have got in your cap, comrade!"

"Who wins one can wear one."

"And may he never repent it!"

The csikós held up his fist with a threatening gesture, till the wide sleeve slipping back disclosed a muscular sunburned arm.

Then both riders putting spurs to their horses went their several ways.

Chapter II

The cowboy trotted towards the herd, and soon the hills of Zám, the little acacia wood, and the three tall well poles began to peep above the horizon. But it is a good ride there! Presently he took the tell-tale rose from his cap, folded it in his scarlet handkerchief, and pushed it up the knotted sleeve of his coat.

The horse-herd meanwhile spurred his horse in the opposite direction, where a low lying line of bluish mist marked the course of the Hortobágy river. He was on his way to the rose-bush where the yellow roses grew.

For on the whole Hortobágy there was but one yellow rose, and that bloomed in the innkeeper's garden.

Some foreigner had brought it from Belgium, they said; and its wonderful yellow flowers blossomed the whole summer through, from Whitsuntide to Advent, when there were still buds on the branches; yellow as pure gold they were, though their scent was more like muscatel wine than roses. Many a man had felt that scent rise to his head! And the girl who used to gather these roses, though not for herself, they called "The Yellow Rose" also.

It was quite a mystery where the old innkeeper had picked up this maiden, for wife he had none. Some stranger had evidently forgotten her there, and the old man had kept her till she grew into a delicate, slender flower. Her cheeks were not rosy like those of other girls, but a clear, creamy color, not the tint of sickness, for the life glowed beneath, and, when she smiled, seemed to dazzle and shine like a fire within. Her mouth, with its turned-up corners, was made for laughter, and suited the darkness of her eyes, eyes so dark that none could tell whether they were black or blue, because if once a man looked into them he forgot all else in the world. Her hair was black, twisted into a plait, with yellow ribbon. Other girls damp their hair with quince juice to make it curly, but hers waved and curled of itself.

And the songs she knew! How sweetly she could sing when she liked! If happy she sang, if sad she sang, for there is a song for everything, and, without singing, a peasant maiden cannot live. Nothing makes the work so easy, the time pass so quickly, and the way so short. Early in the morning, when the sky was pink at sunrise, she might be heard singing as she weeded in the garden.

The old innkeeper did not concern himself with business, but had given the whole management of the inn into the girl's hands. She served out the wine, cooked, did the accounts. He meanwhile looked after his beehives, and was busy now, for the bees were swarming.

Suddenly a horse's hoofs resounded from the yard, the dogs barked in the joyous tone with which they were wont to greet an old friend, and the old man called out:

"Klári! go in! Don't you hear the dogs barking; a customer must be here. See to him!"

The girl dropped her striped gown, tucked up for weeding, put on her buckled shoes, washed her hands from the watering can, and dried them with her apron, which she then threw aside, for, under it, she wore another very wide and clean, and with the household keys dangling from her waistband. She untied her gay-colored kerchief, and smoothed her hair with her moistened palms. Then she broke off a rose from the rose-bush, and stuck it in her hair at one side.

"Picking a rose again!" grumbled the old man. "Maybe only for a gendarme!"

"Why only? Why mayn't a gendarme wear a rose in his shako as well as another fellow? Perhaps you don't think him good enough? That depends on the gendarme."

But after all it was no gendarme whom the girl found sitting at one end of the long table, but the smartest csikós on the whole puszta – Sándor Decsi.

"Sándor!" screamed the girl when she saw him, and clapping her hands, "Sándor! you have come back, my darling."

He was standing there, drumming on the table with the empty glasses, and only looked up to call out in a most sullen fashion, "Bring wine."

"Sándor!" cried the girl.

But the lad only growled, "I told you to bring wine," and let his head fall back on his hands.

"That is a nice 'good morning' after such a long absence!" exclaimed the girl, at which the herdsman came somewhat to his senses, for he knew how to be polite. Removing his cap and laying it on the table, "Good morning, miss," he said.

"Whew!" The girl pointed the rosy tip of her tongue at him, and shrugging her shoulders angrily, stamped off to the bar, shaking her shoes as she went. When she had brought the wine, however, she asked in an unaltered voice:

"Why do you call me 'miss'?"

"Because. . . . you are 'miss.'"

"I always was, but you never used to say so."

"That was another time, it was different then."

"Well, here is the wine anyway. Do you want anything else?"

"Thank you," said the man, "not now. Later perhaps."

The girl responded by a clicking noise with her tongue, and then sat down near him, at the end of the long bench.

The csikós raised the bottle to his lips, drained it dry, and flung it on the floor, where it smashed into a thousand fragments.

"Why have you broken the bottle?" she asked softly.

"That no one else may drink out of it." Next he tossed three ten kreuzer notes on the table – "dog tongues" the country people call them – two being for the red wine, one for the bottle. The girl meanwhile had seized a broom, and was diligently sweeping up the broken glass. Then, knowing the rule, she dived behind the wooden lattice railing off the bar, and brought out a fresh bottle. How she longed to look in his eyes! But he, evidently guessing it, pulled his hat lower over his face than before. Finally, she did manage to get possession of his cap, and then tried to transfer the yellow rose in her hair to the silk ribbon decorating its brim. But the herdsman saw, and snatched it out of her hands.

"Keep your roses for some worthier person," he said shortly.

"Sándor," began the girl at last, "do you wish to make me cry?"

"That would be false, as your words are false. Did not Ferko Lacza leave you this morning with one of your roses in his cap?"

She did not turn red at this, only so much the paler.

"God knows I –"

But a hand laid across her mouth stopped all further speech.

"Do not take God's name in vain!" cried the herdsman; "and how did those golden earrings get into your ears, I wonder?"

"You donkey!" Klári laughed outright. "You gave them to me yourself, only I had them gilded by the jeweler in Újváros."

Then the csikós caught hold of both her hands, and spoke his mind slowly and earnestly. "Dearest Klári," he said, "I won't call you 'miss' anymore – I beg you from the bottom of my heart not to lie to me. Nothing is so detestable as lying. They say, 'lying dog,' though dogs never lie; for a dog has a different bark when he smells a thief round the farm, or scents danger, or hears his master coming, and his bark never misleads. A dog is honest enough, it is men who know how to lie, and theirs is the true yelping. As for me, it never came into my mind to lie, my tongue is not fashioned that way. Lying ill-suits a moustache, and it's a bad business when bearded lips speak lying words like a coward who fears a beating. Now, see, when the conscription was here last autumn, they summoned us all from the puszta. But the townspeople wanted to keep us, for, without herdsmen the cattle and horses would fare badly. So, first they took care to cross the palms of the committee with silver, and then the doctors whispered to us what sort of bodily defect we could feign, so as to be discharged as unfit. Ferko Lacza took to the trick! He swore he was as deaf as a doorpost, could not hear a trumpet even; he, who has such good ears that if a beast lows in the blackest midnight, he can tell whether it is a stray one wandered in among the herd or a cow calling her lost calf. My eyes nearly fell out of my head! Eh, he knew how to lie, the scoundrel! When my turn came to be inspected they made out that my heart beat irregularly. 'Well, if it beats irregularly,' said I, 'it is not my heart that's in fault, but the Yellow Rose yonder, at the Hortobágy inn.' The gentlemen all nudged me to trust to the doctor, who said I had enlargement of the heart! 'Why, it's just big enough to hold one little bit of a girl, and nothing else. There is nothing in the world the matter with me!' So they took me for a soldier, but respected me. They never even cut my hair, but sent me to be 'soldier csikós' to the military stud at Mezöhegyes. And before half a year was over the Town Council put down the thousand florins ransom to buy me off, and send me back to the horses again. But I will work out those thousand florins with my two hands, though not with a lying tongue – that is another matter!"

The girl attempted to get her hands free, and to turn off the affair as a joke.

"My word, Sándor, did you learn to preach when you were eating the Emperor's bread? Really, you're so eloquent you ought to go as probationer every Sunday to Balmaz-Újváros!"

"Now, now, do not jest," said the man. "I know what is in your little head. You are thinking that maids are but a feeble folk, and have no other weapon but lying, otherwise they would be overmatched. The swift feet for the hare, the wings for the bird, and for the girl – her lying lips! But, sweetheart, I am a man who has never hurt the weaker. The hare can bide in the cover, and the bird on her nest for me, I would never disturb them. Neither would I harm the girl who speaks the truth with as much as a hard word or look. But if you lie to me, why, then I must judge you as hardly as if those pretty cheeks of yours were smeared with Vienna rouge! Look at the rose in your hand, it has hardly opened, but if I blow on it with my hot breath, one after another all the petals will unfold. Be such a rose, then, my darling, and open your heart and your soul to me. I will not be angry whatever you confess, and I will forgive you, even if it breaks my heart."

"And then what will you give me?"

"As much of it as you have left me," said the man.

The girl, knowing the herdsmen's custom of eating bacon, paprika (the red pepper), and white bread with their morning wine, rose, and set this before him, and was glad to see it was not scorned. Indeed, the csikós, drawing out his long knife with its inlaid handle from his top boot, cut off a slice of bread and bacon, and fell to work heartily.

Meanwhile, through the open door appeared the watchdog, wagging his tail, and going to the herdsman, he rubbed his nose against his legs, and then lay down near him, yawning with great affability.

"Even Bodri knows you," said the girl.

"Yes, dogs are faithful. It is only girls who forget."

"Sándor, Sándor," she cried. "What a pity it was you could not tell that one little lie when it was so needful! Then they would not have taken you as a soldier to Mezöhegyes. It is not wise to leave a girl to herself. It is not wise to let a lilac-bush in blossom overhang the paling, because then every passer-by who chooses can break off a piece!"

At these words the very morsel of bread fell from the herdsman's mouth, and he cast it to the dog.

"Is this truth that you are saying?"

"Truth? Don't you know the song about 'When the girl's out in the storm, under his cloak the boy keeps her warm'?"

"Yes, and how it goes on too. 'The maid keeps near to the lad in the showers, his cloak being worked with silken flowers.' Get away, dog! Even you only wag your tail when there is a question of bacon!"

Just then the horse in the yard outside began to neigh, and the girl went out, reappearing in a few minutes.

"Where have you been?" asked the man.

"Tying up your horse in the stable."

"Who bid you tie him up?"

"I always did so till now."

"Now it is different; I am off directly!"

"What? You won't take a bite? Isn't bread and bacon good enough? Maybe you got better from the Emperor? But stop, I can bring you something nicer."

She went to the cupboard in the wall and brought out a plate of fried fowl, or "Back Hendli" – for fowl fried in bread-crumbs, and then left cold, was a favorite tit-bit of the herdsman's.

"Whose remains are these?" he demanded suspiciously.

"Well, first think a little! All sorts of people come to an inn, and anyone who pays can have 'Back Hendli.'"

"Then you had grand folks here last night?"

"Certainly," said the girl. "Two gentlemen from Vienna, and two from Debreczin. They stayed up till two o'clock and then went on. If you don't believe me, I can show you their names in the guest book."

"Oh! I believe you."

The great tabby Tom, who had been washing his face by the stove, rose at this moment, stretched himself, arched his back, jumped down, and going to the csikós, measured his claws on his boots, showing how high the snow would lie next winter.

Then he sprang into his friend's arms, rubbing and pushing his head against his hand, and slowly licking everyone of the five fingers. At last he lay down and began purring.

"Look how the cat is trying to coax you," said Klári.

"I am not going to ask him whose arms he purred in yesterday. How much do I pay for the 'Back Hendli'?"

"*You!* Nothing, of course, somebody else did that. But where are you off to in such a terrible hurry?"

"To the vet, on the Mata puszta – I am taking him a letter."

"You won't find him at home, for he passed here at three this morning, looking for those gentlemen. When he heard they had gone, he went jogging on in his gig to the Zám puszta. One gentleman was the steward of a Moravian Count, who wants to buy some of our cattle to breed on his estate; the other German was an artist. He drew me in his little book, and the cowherd also."

"So the cowherd was here also?"

"Of course he was here, since he was sent to show the gentlemen across the puszta to the Zám Herd."

"Only it seems funny to me," remarked the csikós, "that the cowboy left an hour later than the gentlemen he was meant to guide."

"Dear me! You can cross-examine like the district judge! Well, he came to bid me good-bye. He is going far away, and we will never see him anymore."

As if to prove the truth of her words, a real shining tear dropped from the girl's eyes, though she tried her best to hide it. Not that the csikós minded that, for it was an honest tear, at any rate, and he preferred to turn his head aside when she dried her eyes with her apron. Then he stuck his short clay pipe in his mouth. A pipe in the mouth signifies no kisses.

"And what takes the cowboy so far away?" he inquired.

"He is going to Moravia as head herdsman to the cattle which they are buying at Zám. He is to get a stone house, so much corn, and six hundred florins as wages. He'll be quite the gentleman! And they will respect him there, because only a Hungarian herdsman can manage a Hungarian herd."

"And you? Aren't you going to Moravia as head herdsman's wife?"

"You rascal!" said the girl. "You know I'm not. You know, quite well, I love no one but you. I might if I weren't chained fast to you and to this puszta. Why, I am your slave."

"Not exactly," said the man. "You know it is not like that; but whoever you have bewitched with those eyes of yours must come back from the ends of the earth to you. You give him a charm to drink that compels him to think of you. Or you sew one of your hairs in his shirt sleeve, that you may draw him back, even from beyond the stars. It's just the same with me! Since I looked into your eyes I have been made a fool of."

"And have I not been fool enough?" she asked. "Haven't I often wondered what would become of me! Whom did I ask to melt lead with me on Christmas Eve? Whose kerchief did I wear, though he never said it was a betrothal gift? Did I ever go spying after you when you danced with other girls and giddy young wives at Újváros Fair?"

"If only you had not put the rose in his cap!"

"Well, give me yours, and here is a match to it, which is easily stuck in!"

"No," said the lad. "I want *that* rose which you gave to the cowherd, and I will never rest till I have it in my hands."

At that the girl clasped her hands imploringly.

"Sándor! Sándor! Don't talk like that. You two must not fight about me – *about a yellow rose!*"

"It must be. Either he kills me, or I him, but one of us must fall."

"And that is what *you* call telling the truth!" cried the girl. "You who have just promised not to be angry with me anymore?"

"With you, yes. A girl can't help forgetting, but a man should bear in mind."

"God knows, I never forgot you."

"Perhaps not; like in the song: –

"'Whome'er within my arms I pressed,
Yet in my heart I loved thee best.'

"No, dearest, I am not a hard man, and I did not come to quarrel with you, but only to show you that I am alive, and not dead, though I know how happy you would be if I were."

"Sándor! Then you want me to go and buy matches?"

"Matches, is it?" said the man. "That's the way with you girls. If you fall into the ditch, then it's three boxes of matches from the Jew, a cup of hot coffee, and it is all over. But surely the wiser plan would be to avoid the ditches altogether!"

"Don't speak about it. Do you remember," the girl asked, "how, when first we met, we were playing that game, 'I fell into the well. Who pulled you out? Sándor Decsi!' And you did pull me out!"

"But if I had thought it was for someone else. . . !"

"Heigho!" sighed the herdsman, "that was long ago. Before ever the Dorozsma Mill was sung about."

"Is that something new?" The girl stooped over the bench closer to the lad. "Sing it first, and then I will learn it."

So Sándor Decsi set his back against the wall, put one hand to his cap and the other on the table and commenced the tune, the sad air suiting the sadness of its words: –

"Dorozsma's mill, Dorozsma's mill,
The wind has dropped, 'tis standing still.
Ah! faithless thou hast flown, my dove!
Another claims thy life, thy love,
This is the reason, if you will,
Why turns no more Dorozsma's mill."

Such a song it was as is born on the plains and blown hither and thither like the thistledown scattered by the wind. The girl tried the air after him, and where she failed the csikós helped her, and so it went on till they both knew it, and sang it together perfectly. And then, at the finish, they kissed each other. This was the end of the song.

But hardly had Klári sung the last note before Sándor Decsi had stuck the short clay pipe in his mouth again.

"There you go, putting that horrid pipe in your mouth!" she exclaimed sulkily.

"Well, it matches me, I'm horrid too," said the lad.

"You are, just a horrid rascal! A lad like you is good for nothing else but to be turned into a distaff, and stuck up behind the door!"

So saying she gave him a shove with her elbow.

"Now what are you coming round me for?" he asked.

"I coming round you? Do I want you! If lads like you were sold by the dozen, never a one would I buy. I was blind and cracked for sure to have loved you? Why, I could have ten such lads as you for everyone of my ten fingers!"

She stormed in so genuine a manner that at last even Bodri was deceived, and believing that his mistress was offended with this horrid man, jumped up and began growling at him. It made the girl laugh heartily, but the csikós neither caught her merriment nor saw any cause for laughter. He just sat there, moody and silent, holding his pipe between his teeth. The pipe was not alight, for indeed it was empty. Then the girl tried teasing him.

"Well, dear! You are quite aware of your own good looks!" she said, "You wouldn't laugh for the world, would you? Why it would squeeze up your two black eyes, and make your two red lips quite crooked, and all your beauty would be spoiled!"

"Debreczin town does not pay me for being beautiful."

"But I do. Wasn't my payment big enough for you?"

"It was. There was even enough for another person left over."

"Are you beginning again? All about that one yellow rose? Are you so jealous of your comrade then, your own close companion? How could he help himself, poor fellow? If a gallant of the town feels his heart aching for a rose, why he has the whole flower garden to choose from, full of all sorts and shades of roses – red, pink, yellow, and cream! But how does the song go?

"'Only the peasant maid can still
The peasant's heart in good and ill!'"

"So you take his part?"

"Well, whose fault is it? The girl's who sings, 'An' he knew he could, An' he knew it still he would,' or the man's who listens and understands?"

"Do you take the blame then?"

"You said you would forgive me everything."

"I will keep my word."

"And love me again?"

"Later."

"Ah! it's a big word that 'later,'" said the girl.

"I love you now."

"As you have shown me."

The csikós rose from the table, stuck the short pipe into the wide brim of his hat, and going to the girl, put his arms round her, gazing, as he spoke, into her large dark eyes.

"My darling, you know there are two kinds of fever – the hot and the cold. The hot is more violent, but the cold lasts longer; the one passes quickly, the other returns again and again. But I will just speak plainly, and not mince matters. Mine was the fault, for if I had not breathed on my yellow rosebud, it would not have opened, and others would not have found out the sweet scent which has brought all the wasps and moths. I do love you indeed, but differently now, with the constancy of the cold sort of fever. I will deal as truly by you as thine own mother, and as soon as I am made head herdsman we will go to the priest and live faithfully together ever afterwards. But if I find anyone else fluttering around, then God help me, for were he my father's own son, I will crack his head for him. Here's my hand on it." He stretched out his hand to the girl, and she, in answer, pulled out her golden earrings, placing them in his open palm.

"But, dearest, wear them," he insisted, "if as you say they are my silver ones gilded, and I must believe you!"

So she put them back in her ears, and in so doing she put something back in her heart that had lain hidden there till now. Somehow this sort of love, likened to the shivering stage of fever, was not altogether to her taste. She understood the burning fit better.

Next the girl, after reflecting, slipped the cloak from the herdsman's neck and hung it up behind the lattice of the bar, as she was accustomed to take the coats of customers in pledge, who could not pay their reckoning.

"Don't hurry," she said, "there is time. The Vet can't possibly be back at the Mata Farm before noon, because he must examine all the cattle that are sold, and write a certificate for each. You will only find his old housekeeper, and here you are safe and dry. Neither the storm can drench you, nor your sweetheart's tears. Look how glad your last words have made me! They will be in my head all day long."

"And see how far away I thought of those last words, since I have brought you a present. It is in my cloak sleeve yonder, go and fetch it out."

Many things were in that sleeve – steel, flint, and tinder, tobacco pouch, money bag, and among it all the girl discovered a new packet, done up in silver paper. When it was unfolded, and she beheld a comb of yellow tortoise-shell, her face beamed with happiness.

"This is for *me?*"

"Whom *else?*"

Now when a peasant maid twists her plait of hair round a comb, it means she is betrothed, has a lover of her own, and is "ours" no longer. Nor can she anymore sing the song about "I know not whose darling am I."

Standing before the mirror, Klári "did up" her hair in a knot round the comb, and then she looked prettier than ever.

"Now you shall kiss me," she said. She offered the kiss herself in fact, stretching out her arms, but the man held her back.

"Not yet," he said, "I will be hot presently, but I am still shivering."

It was a rebuff, and the girl drew her brows together, for she felt shamed, and besides something burned in her heart. However, she only tried harder to be loving and gentle, love and anger meanwhile striving madly together in her heart – anger just because of the love.

"Shall I sing your favorite song," she asked, "while the fish is roasting?"

"If you like."

She went to the fireplace, took a fish out of a big barrel full of the Hortobágy fish, called "Kárász," slashed it with a kitchen knife on both sides, sprinkled it well with salt and pepper, and sticking a skewer through it, placed it beside the red hot embers. Then she sang in her sweet, clear voice:

"Ho! good dame of the Puszta Inn,
Bake me fish, bring lemon and wine,
Set your wench on the watch without,
Bid her tell what she sees in time."

The song has a fascination of its own, bringing visions of the endless puszta with the mirage overhanging its horizon, and echoes, too, of the lone shepherd's pipe, and the sad sounding horn of the herdsman. Besides, is not the whole romance of the "betyárs'," the puszta robbers', life contained in the words:

"Set your wench on the watch without,
Bid her tell what she sees in time?"

As soon as the fish was browned enough, the girl brought it to the csikós. Never is this dish eaten otherwise than by holding the end of the spit in the fingers, and picking off the fish with a pocketknife. It tastes best like that, and a girl cannot show her love for her sweetheart more distinctly than by roasting him a fish on the spit. Then what a delight it is to watch him enjoying the work of her hands!

Meanwhile Klári went on singing:

"'Nine gendarmes and their weapons flash!'
Cries the girl in her frightened haste;
But the betyár gallops his swift bay steed
Where the mirage plays o'er the boundless waste."

Once, when they sang this together, at the line "gallops his swift bay steed," the herdsman would throw up his cap to the rafters, and bring down his fist with a crash on the table.

But now he did not heed it.

"Don't you care for the song nowadays?" asked the girl. "Even that doesn't please you?"

"Why should it? I'm no 'betyár,' and have nothing to do with thieves. Gendarmes are honest men, and do their duty. As for a good-for-nothing 'betyár,' he sets a girl to watch outside, and as soon as he sees so much as the tip of a gendarme's helmet, he is off and away, 'O'er the boundless waste,' leaving fish and wine and all behind him. And he shouts it out in his own praise too! The cowardly thief!"

"Well, you *have* changed since you ate the Emperor's bread!"

"I've not changed, but the times. You can turn a coat inside out if you like. After all it is only a coat. A bunda – fur-lined cloak – is always a bunda."

"And do you know," said the girl, "the greatest insult a man can pay his sweetheart is to quote a worn-out old saw like that –"

"But if I know none better! Perhaps the gentlemen from Moravia, who were here last night, had newer jokes to amuse you with?"

"Better jokes!" said the girl. "Anyway they didn't sit here looking like stuck pigs. The painter especially was a very proper young fellow. If he had only been a hair's breadth taller! As it was he just came up to my chin!"

"Did you measure yourselves then?"

"Rather! Why I taught him to dance csárdás, and he jumped about like a two months old kid on the barn floor!"

"And the cowherd?" asked the man, "did he see you dancing with the German artist, and yet not wring his neck?"

"Wring his neck! Why they drank eternal friendship together!"

"Well, it is not my business. Get me some more wine, but better stuff than this vinegar. I shall have to come out with another old saying, 'The fish is unhappy in the third water,' for the third water should be wine."

"That's a double insult to call my wine – water."

"Never mind," said the herdsman, "just get me a sealed bottle!"

Now it was the undoing of Sándor Decsi that he asked for a sealed bottle, one brought from the town, sealed with green wax, with a pink or blue label pasted on one side, covered with golden letters. Such wine is only fit for gentlefolk, or perhaps for people in the Emperor's pay!

Klári's heart beat loud and fast as she went into the cellar to fetch a bottle of this gentlefolk's wine.

For, suddenly, the girl remembered about a gypsy woman, who had once told her fortune for some old clothes, and, out of pure gratitude, had said this to her as well, "Should your lover's heart grow cold, my dear, and you wish to make it flame again, that is easily managed, give him wine mixed with lemon juice, and drop a bit of this root called 'fat mannikin' into it.

Then his love will blaze up again, till he would break down walls to reach you!"

It flashed across the girl's mind that now was the very moment to test the charm, and the roots, stumpy and black, like little round-headed, fat-legged mannikins, were lying safe in a drawer of her chest. In the olden days much was believed of this magic plant, how it shrieked when pulled from the ground, and that those who heard it died. How, at last, they took dogs to uproot it, tying them to it by the tail! How Circe bewitched Ulysses and his comrades with it. The chemist, who has another use for it, calls it "atropa mandragora." But how could the girl know that it was poisonous?

Chapter III

Early, ere the dawn, the strangers at the Hortobágy inn started on their way.

This inn, though only a "csárda," or wayside house of call, was no owl-haunted, tumble-down, reed-thatched place, such as the painter had imagined, but a respectable brick building, with a shingle roof, comfortable rooms, and a capital kitchen and cellar quite worthy of any town. Below the flower garden, the Hortobágy river wound silently along, between banks fringed with reeds and willows. Not far from the inn, the high road crossed it on a substantial stone bridge of nine arches. Debreczin folk maintain that the solidity of this bridge is due to the masons having used milk to slake their lime; jealous people say that they employed wine made from Hortobágy grapes, and that this drew it together.

The object of the early start was æsthetic as well as practical. The painter looked forward to seeing a sunrise on the puszta, a sight which no one, who has not viewed it with his own eyes, can form the slightest idea of. The practical reason was that the cattle to be sold could only be separated from the herd in the early morning. In spring, most of them have little calves, and at dawn, when these are not sucking, the herdsmen going in among the herd, catch those whose mothers have been selected and take them away. The mothers then follow of their own accord. A stranger would be gored to death by these wild creatures, who have never seen anyone but their own drovers, but to them they are quite accustomed.

So the strangers set off for those wild parts of the plain, where even the puszta dwellers need a guide, in a couple of light carriages. The two coachmen, however, knew the district, and needed no pilot. They therefore left the cowboy, who had been sent as guide, to amuse himself at the inn, he promising to overtake them before they reached the herd.

The artist was a famous landscape painter from Vienna, who often came to Hungary for the sake of his work, and who spoke the tongue of the people. The other Viennese was manager of the stables to the Moravian landowner, Count Engelshort. It would, perhaps, have been wiser to have sent some farmer who knew about cattle, for a lover of horses has little mind left for anything else. But he had this advantage over the rest of the staff, that he knew Hungarian, for when a lieutenant of Dragoons he had long been stationed in Hungary, where the fair ladies had taught him to speak it. Two of the Count's drovers had been told off to escort him – strong, sturdy fellows, each armed with a revolver. As for the gentlemen from Debreczin, one was the chief constable, the other the worthy citizen from whose herd the twenty-four stock cows and their bull were to be selected.

Now, at the time of starting, the waning moon and the brightest of the stars were still visible, while over in the east dawn was already breaking.

The townsman, a typical Magyar, explained to the painter how the star above them was called "the wanderer's lamp," and how the "poor lads," or "betyárs," looking up at it, would sigh, "God help us," and so escape detection when stealing cattle. This quite enchanted the painter.

"What a Shakespearian idea," he said.

He grew more and more impressed with the endless vision of puszta, when, an hour later, their galloping steeds brought them where nothing could be seen save sky above and grass below, where there was not a bird or frog-eating stork to relieve the marvelous monotony.

"What tones! What tints! What harmony in the contrasts!"

"It's all well enough," said the farmer, "till the mosquitoes and the horse-flies come."

"And that fresh, velvety turf, against those dark pools!"

"Those puddles there? 'Tocsogo' as we call them."

Meanwhile, high above, sounded the sweet song of the lark.

"Ah, those larks; how wonderful, how splendid!"

"They're thin enough now, but wait till the wheat ripens," replied the farmer.

Slowly the light grew, the purple of the sky melted into gold; the morning star, herald of the sun, already twinkled above the now visible horizon, and a rainbowlike iridescence played over the dewy grass, keeping pace with the movements of the dark figures. The horses, four to each carriage, flew over the pathless green meadow-land, till, presently, something began to show dark on the horizon – a plantation, the first acacias on the hitherto treeless puszta, and some bluish knolls.

"Those are the Tartar hills of Zám," explained the Debreczin farmer to his companions. "There stood some village destroyed by the Tartars. The ruins of the church still peep out of the grass, and the dogs, when they dig holes, scrape out human bones."

"And there, what sort of a Golgotha is that?"

"That," said the farmer, "is no Golgotha, but the three poles of the cattle wells. We are close to the herd."

They halted at the acacias, and there agreed to await the doctor who was to come jogging along from the Mata puszta, in his one-horse trap. Meanwhile the painter made notes in his sketch-book, falling from ecstasy to ecstasy. "What subjects! What motives!" In vain his companions urged him to draw a fine solitary acacia, rather than a group of nasty old thistles! At last appeared the doctor and his gig, coming up from a slanting direction, but he did not stop, only shouted "Good morning" from the box, and then, "Hurry, hurry! before the daylight comes!" So after a long enough drive they reached "the great herd." This is the pride of the Hortobágy puszta – one thousand five hundred cattle all in one mass. Now all lay silent, but whether sleeping or not, who could tell? No one has ever seen cattle with closed eyes and heads resting on the ground, and to them Hamlet's soliloquy, "To sleep, perchance to dream," in no wise applies.

"What a picture!" cried the painter, enchanted. "A forest of uplifted horns, and there in the middle the old bull himself with his sooty head and his wrinkled neck. The jet black litter surrounded by green pasture, the grey mist in the background, and, far away, the light of a shepherd's fire! This must be perpetuated!"

Thereupon he sprang from the carriage, saying, "Please follow the others. I see the shelter, and will meet you there." So, taking his paint-box and camp-stool, and laying his sketch-book on his knees, he began rapidly jotting down the scene, while the carriage with the farmer drove on.

All at once, the two watchdogs of the herd, observing this strange figure on the puszta, rushed towards him, barking loudly. It was, however, not the painter's way to be frightened. The dogs, moreover, with their white coats and black noses, fell into the scheme of color. Nor did they attack the man, peacefully squatting there, but when quite close to him, stood still. "What could he be?" Sitting down, they poked out their heads inquisitively at the sketch-book. "What was this?" The painter pursued the joke, for he daubed the cheek of the one with green, and the other with pink; and these attentions they seemed to find flattering, but when they by-and-by saw each other's pink or green face, they fancied it was that of a strange dog, and took to fighting.

Luckily the "taligás," or wheel-barrow boy, came up at that moment. The taligás is the youngest boy on the place, and his duty is to follow the cattle with his wheel-barrow, and scrape up the "poor man's peat" which they leave on the meadow. This serves as fuel on the puszta, and its smoke is alike grateful to the nose of man and beast.

The taligás rushed his barrow between the fighting dogs, separated and pursued them, shouting, "Get away there!" For the puszta watchdog does not fear the stick, but of the wheel-barrow he is in terror.

The taligás was a very smart little lad, in his blue shirt and linen breeches worked with scarlet. He delivered the message entrusted to him by the gentlemen, very clearly. It was "that the painter should join them at the shelter, where there was much to sketch." But the striking picture of the herd was not yet completed.

"Can you run me along in your barrow?" asked the painter, "for this silver piece?"

"Oh, sir!" said the lad, "I've wheeled a much heavier calf than you! Please step in, sir."

So utilising this clever idea, the painter gained both his ends. He got to the "karám," seated in the barrow, and managed to finish his characteristic sketch by the way.

Meanwhile the others had left their carriages, and were introducing the Vienna cattle buyer to the herdsman in charge. This man was an exceptionally fine example of the Hungarian puszta-dweller. A tall, strong fellow, with hair beginning to turn grey, and a curled and waxed moustache. His face was bronzed from exposure to hard weather, and his eyebrows drawn together from constant gazing into the sun.

By "Karám" is understood on the puszta that whole arrangement which serves as shelter against wind and storm for both man and beast. Wind is the great enemy. Rain, heat, and cold the herdsman ignores. He turns his fur-lined cloak inside out, pulls down his cap, and faces it, but against wind he needs protection, for wind is a great power on the plains. Should the whirlwind catch the herd on the pastures, it will, unless there be some wood to check them, drive them straight to the Theiss. So the shelter is formed of a planking of thick boards, with three extended wings into the corners of which the cattle can withdraw.

The herdsmen's dwelling is a little hut, its walls plastered like a swallow's nest. It is not meant for sleeping in, there is not room enough, but is only a place where the men keep their furs and their "bank." This is just a small calf's skin with the feet left on, and a lock in place of the head. It holds their tobacco, red pepper, even their papers. Round the walls hang their cloaks, the embroidered "szür" for summer, for winter the fur-lined bunda. These are the herdsman's coverings, and in them he sleeps beneath God's sky. Only the overseer reposes under the projecting eaves, on a wooden bench for bedstead, above his head the shelf with the big round loaves, and the tub that holds the week's provisions. His wife, who lives in the town, brings them every Sunday afternoon.

Before the hut stands a small circular erection woven out of reeds, with a brick-paved flooring and no roof. This is the kitchen, the "vásalo," and here the herdsman's stew, "gulyáshús" and meal porridge are cooked in a big pot hung on a forked stick. The taligás does the cooking. A row of long-handled tin spoons are stuck in the reed wall.

"But where did the gentlemen leave the cowboy?" asked the overseer.

"He had some small account to settle with the innkeeper's daughter," answered the farmer. His name was Sajgató.

"Well, if he comes home drunk the betyár!"

"Betyár," interrupted the painter, delighted at hearing the word. "Is our cowboy a betyár?"

"I only used the expression as a compliment," the overseer explained.

"Ah!" sighed the painter, "I should so like to see a *real* betyár, to put him in my sketch-book!"

"Well, the gentleman won't find one here, we don't care for thieves. If one comes roaming around we soon kick him out."

"So there are no betyárs left on the Hortobágy puszta?"

"There's no saying! Certainly there are plenty of thieves among the shepherds, and some of the swineherds turn brigands, and it does sometimes happen that when a csikós gets silly and loses his head, he sinks to a vagabond betyár, but no one can ever remember a cowboy having taken to robbery."

"How is that?"

"Because the cowboy works among quiet, sensible beasts. He never sits drinking with shepherds and swineherds."

"Then the cowherd is the aristocrat of the puszta?" remarked the manager of the stables.

"That's it, exactly. Just as counts and barons are among grand folk, so are csikós and cowboys among the other herdsmen."

"So there is no equality on the puszta?"

"As long as men are on the earth, there will never be equality," said the overseer. "He who is born a gentleman will remain one, even in a peasant's coat. He will never steal his neighbor's cow or horse, even if he find it straying, but will drive it back to its owner. But whether he won't try a little cheating at the market, that I am not prepared to say."

"For gentlemen to take in each other at the horse fair is, however, quite an aristocratic custom!"

"Still more so at the cattle market, so I would recommend you to use your eyeglass while you are with us, for when once you have driven off your cattle I am no longer responsible."

"Thanks for the warning," said the manager.

Here the doctor interrupted the discussion.

"Come out, gentlemen," he cried, "in front of the kitchen, and see the sunrise."

The painter rushed forward, and began to sketch, but soon fell into utter despair.

"Why, this is absurd! What color! dark blue ground, violet mist on the horizon, above it orange sky, and over that a long streak of rosy cloud. What, a purple glory announces the coming of the sun! A glowing fire is rising above the sharply defined horizon! Just like a burning pyramid, now like red hot iron! Yet not so dazzling that one cannot look at it with the naked eye. Now look, do! The sun is five-sided, the upper part grows egg-shaped! The lower contracts, the top flattens out, now it is quite like a mushroom! No, no, a Roman urn. This is absurd, it can't be painted. Now there comes a thin cloud which turns it into a blindfolded cupid, or a bearded deputy. No! If I painted the sun five-sided and with a moustache they would shut me up in an asylum."

The painter threw down his brushes.

"These Hungarians," he said, "must always have something out of the common. Here they are giving us a sunrise which is a reality, but at the same time an impossibility. That is not as it should be."

The doctor began to explain that this was only an optical delusion, like the *fata morgana,* and was due to the refraction of the rays through the differently heated strata of the atmosphere.

"All the same it is impossible," said the painter. "Why, I can't believe what I see."

But the sun did not leave him in wonder much longer. Hitherto, the whole display had been but a dazzling effect of mirage, and when the real orb rose with floods of light, the human eye could no longer gaze at it with impunity. Then the rosy heavens suddenly brightened into gold, and the line of the horizon appeared to melt into the sky.

At the first flash of sunlight the whole sleeping camp stirred. The forest of horns of fifteen hundred cattle moved. The old bull shook the bell at his neck, and at its sound uprose the puszta chorus. One thousand five hundred cattle began to low.

"Splendid! Good Lord," exclaimed the painter ecstatically. "This is a Wagner chorus! Oboes, hunting horns, kettledrums! What an overture! What a scene! It is a finale from the Götterdämmerung!"

"Yes, yes," said Mr. Sajgató. "But now they are going to the well. Every cow is calling her calf, that is why they are lowing."

Three herdsmen ran to the well – the beam of which testified to the skill of the carpenter – and setting the three buckets in motion, emptied the water into the large drinking trough – fatiguing work which has to be done three times a day.

"Would it not be simpler to use some mechanism worked by horse-power?" inquired the German gentleman of the overseer.

"We have such a machine," he replied, "but the cowboy would rather wear out his own hands than frighten his horse with it."

Meanwhile a fourth cowboy had been occupied in picking out those cows which belonged to Mr. Sajgató, and in removing their calves, which he drove into the corral, the mothers following them meekly into the fenced enclosure.

"These are mine," said Mr. Sajgató.

"But how can the herdsman tell among a thousand cattle which belong to Mr. Sajgató?" asked the manager of the stables. "How do you know one from the other?"

The overseer cast a compassionate glance over his shoulder at the questioner.

"Has the gentleman ever seen two cows just alike?"

"To my eyes they are all alike."

"But not to the herdsman's," said the overseer.

The manager, however, professed himself perfectly satisfied with the selected cattle.

The barrow-boy now came up, and announced that from the look-out tree he had seen the other cowherd coming up at a gallop.

"Running his horse!" growled the overseer. "Just let him show his face here. I'll thrash him till he forgets even his own name."

"But you won't really strike him?"

"No, for whoever beats a cowherd will have to kill him before he cures him in that way, and he's my favorite lad too! I brought him up and christened him. He is my godson, the rascal!"

"Yet you part with him? He is taking the herd to Moravia!"

"Yes," said the overseer. "Just because I have a leaning towards the boy. I don't like the way he is going on – head over ears in love with that pale-faced girl at the Hortobágy inn. 'Tis a bad business. The girl has a sweetheart already. A csikós, who is away soldiering; and if he comes home on leave and the lads meet, it will be like two angry bulls who mean business. Much better that he should go away and take to some pretty little Annie up there, and forget all about his yellow rose."

In the meantime the veterinary had examined every beast separately, and had made out a certificate for each. Then the taligás marked the buyer's initials in vermilion on their hides – for all the herdsmen can write.

The clattering hoofs of the horse which carried the cowboy could now be heard. His sleepiness had vanished with the sharp ride, and the morning air had cleared his head. He sprang smartly from the saddle, at some distance from the corral, and came up leading his horse by the bridle.

"You rag-tag and bobtail!" called out the overseer from the front of the enclosure. "Where the devil have you been?"

Not a word said the lad, but slipped the saddle and bridle off his horse. It was white with foam, and taking a corner of his coat he rubbed its chest, wiped it down, and fastened on the halter.

"Where were you? by Pontius Pilate's copper angel! Coming an hour behind the gentry you should have brought with you. Eh, scoundrel?"

Still the lad was silent, fiddled with the horse, and hung saddle and bridle on the rack.

The overseer's face grew purple. He screamed the louder, "Will you answer me, or shall I have to bore a hole in your ears?"

Then the cowboy spoke. "You know, master, that I am deaf and dumb."

"Damn the day you were born!" cried the overseer. "Do you think I invented that story that you should mock me? Don't you see the sun is up?"

"Well, is it my fault that the sun is up?"

The others began to laugh, while the overseer's wrath increased.

"Take care, you blackguard, better not attempt to trifle with me, for if I once lay hands on you, I'll mangle you like unbleached linen."

"I'll be there too, you bet!"

"Indeed you won't, rascal," exclaimed the overseer, who himself could not help laughing. "There! talk to him in German any of you who can!"

The manager of the stables thereupon thought he might have a talk with the herdsman in German.

"You're a fine strong fellow!" he said, "I wonder they didn't make an Hussar of you. Why did they not enlist you? What defect could they find?"

The cowboy made a wry grimace, for peasant lads do not much care for those sort of questions.

"I think they did not take me for a soldier," he answered, "because there are two holes in my nose."

"There, you see, he can't talk sense!" exclaimed the overseer. "Clear out, you betyár, to the watering – not there! What did I tell you? Are you tipsy? Can't you see the cows are all corralled, and who is to bring out the bull?"

It takes a man, and no mere stripling, to take a bull out of the herd, and this Ferko Lacza was a master of the art. With sweet words and caresses, such as he might use to a pet lamb, he coaxed out the beast which belonged to Mr. Sajgató, and led him in front of the gentlemen. A splendid animal he was too; massive head, sharp horns, and great black-ringed eyes. There he stood, allowing the cowboy to scratch his shaggy forehead, and licking his hand with his rough, rasping tongue.

"And the beast has only seen the third grass," said its owner. The herdsmen reckon the age of their cattle according to the grass, that is the summers they have lived through.

Meanwhile the painter did not let slip the opportunity of making a sketch of the great horned beast and its companion. "The cowboy must stand just like that with his hand on the horns." The lad, however, was not used to posing, and it injured his dignity.

When their models are restless, artists often try and amuse them with conversation.

"Tell me," asked the painter – the others were inspecting the cows – "is it true that you herdsmen can cheat about your cattle at the market?"

"Why, yes. The master has this very moment taken in the gentleman with the bull. He made it out to be three years old, and see, there is not an eye tooth left in its head!" He opened the animal's mouth as he spoke to prove the fact of the deception.

The painter's sense of honor was even keener than his passion for art. He immediately stopped painting. "I have finished," he said, and hastily closing his sketch-book, he departed in search of his friends, who were standing among the chosen cattle in the enclosure. Then he revealed the great secret. The manager of the stables was horror-struck. Opening the mouths of two or three cows, he called out:

"Look here, overseer! You warned us that cattle sellers like to 'green' their customers, but I won't be done like this. Everyone of these cows is so old that there is not an eye tooth left in its head."

The overseer stroked his moustache, and answered with a broad grin, "Yes, I know that joke; it came out in last year's calendar. The General who was cheated in the Franco-Prussian War through not knowing that cattle have no eye teeth."

"Haven't they?" asked the manager in surprise, and when the doctor assured him that it was so, he said petulantly, "Well, how should I know about a cow's mouth? I am no cattle dentist. All my work has lain among horses!" But he must needs vent his anger on somebody, so he flew upon the painter for having led him into such a trap. "How could you?" he demanded. The painter, however, was too much of a gentleman to betray the cowboy, who had first taken him in. At last the taligás put an end to the dispute by respectfully announcing that breakfast was waiting.

The taligás is cook on the puszta. All this time he had been preparing the herdsman's breakfast of "tesztás kása," or meal porridge. Now, bringing out the pot, he set it on a three-legged stool. The guests sat round it, and to each he handed a long tin spoon with which to help himself. "Excellent," pronounced the gentlemen, and when they had eaten, the overseer and the herdsmen devoured what remained. The scrapings of the pot fell to the taligás. Meanwhile, Mr. Sajgató was in the kitchen preparing the "Hungarian coffee," which all who have been on the puszta know so well. "Hungarian coffee" is red wine heated up with brown sugar, cinnamon, and cloves. It tastes most delicious after such an early outing on the plains.

Then the taligás took the pot, rinsed it, filled it with water, and hung it over the fire. The gulyás stew would be ready when the gentlemen returned from their walk. They would then taste something really good!

Ferko Lacza showed the company round, pointing out to the strangers all the sights of the puszta, such as the wind shelter and the railed-in burying place for cattle.

"In the good old days," he explained, "if a beast died, we just left it where it fell, and the vultures came in flocks and picked it clean. Now, since this new order has come out, we have to inform the vet over at the Mata Farm, who comes and inspects it, writes down what it died of, and bids us bury it without fail. But we are sorry to see so much good meat wasted, so we manage to take a chunk or two, which we cut up small, cook, and spread out in the sun to dry. This we stuff into our bags, and whenever we want gulyás, why we throw as many dried handfuls of meat into the pot as there are men to eat it."

The painter looked the cowboy hard in the face, then turned to his master.

"Does this worthy herdsman of yours ever happen to speak the truth, overseer?"

"Very rarely, but this time he has, for once in his life."

"Then thank you very much for your delightful gulyás."

"Oh don't be alarmed!" said the overseer, "there's nothing bad about it. Since God laid out the flat Hortobágy, that has always been the custom. Look at those lads, can you desire healthier or stronger fellows? Yet they have all grown up on carrion. The learned professors may talk as much as they like, it doesn't hurt us Hungarians."

The manager, however, listening to this revelation, strictly forbade his Moravian drovers to touch the dish.

"Though who knows," said the painter, "whether the old humbug has not invented the whole story to scare us from the feast, and then have a good laugh at us!"

"We'll see," rejoined his comrade, "whether the vet eats it or not, for he must know all about it."

And now came the mirage, that seems like the realization of a fairy dream.

Along the horizon lay a quivering sea, where high waves chased each other from east to west, the real hills standing out as little islands in their midst, and the stumpy acacias magnified into vast forests. Oxen, grazing in the distance, were transformed into a street of palaces. Boats which appeared to cross the ocean turned out on reaching the shore to be nothing but some far off horses. The fantastic deception is always at its height directly after sunrise, when whole villages are often raised into the air, and brought so close that, with a glass, the carts in their streets can be distinguished, their towers and houses being all mirrored upside down on the billowy fairy sea. During cloudy weather, however, they remain below the horizon.

"Let the Germans copy this," exclaimed Mr. Sajgató to the admiring group, while the painter tore his hair in despair.

"Why am I compelled to see things I can't put on canvas? What *is* this?"

"Why the mirage," said the overseer.

"And what is the mirage?"

"The mirage is the mirage of the Hortobágy."

But Ferko Lacza knew more than his master.

"The mirage is God's miracle," he told them, "sent to keep us poor herdsmen from growing weary of the long day on the puszta."

Finally the painter turned to the doctor for an explanation. "I know even less," said he. "I have read Flammarion's book on the atmosphere, where he speaks of the Fata Morgana as seen on the African deserts, the coasts of the Arctic ocean, on the Orinoco, and in Sicily, also Humboldt and Bompland's descriptions. But learned men know nothing of the Hortobágy mirage, though it may be seen every hot summer's day from sunrise to sundown. Thus are Hungary's wonderful natural phenomena utterly ignored by the scientific world."

It did the doctor good to pour out the bitterness of his heart before the strangers, but he had no time to admire the marvels of nature, being obliged to hurry back to his animal hospital and pharmacy at Mata. So, bidding adieu to both his old and new friends, he jumped into his gig, and jogged away over the plain.

The herd was already scattered far out on the puszta, the cowboys driving it forward. The grass near at hand is more luscious, but in spring the cattle graze far afield, so that when summer scorches the distant pastures, the nearer still remain for them. Very touching was the farewell between the main herd and their companions in the enclosure – like a chorus of Druids and Valkyre.

The head of the stables had meanwhile been occupied with the financial side of the business and in arranging the line of march. In crisp brand new hundred florin notes he paid Mr. Sajgató, who stuffed them into his pocket so carelessly, that the manager thought it not superfluous to remind him to look after his money on the puszta. Whereupon the proud citizen of Debreczin answered phlegmatically,

"Sir, I have been plundered and deceived during the course of my existence, but never by robbers or rogues. They were always 'honorable gentlemen,' who knew how to thieve and cheat!"

The overseer likewise received his fee. "If," said the old herdsman, "I might – out of pure friendliness – give you a word of advice, I would recommend you, as you have bought the cows, to take the calves as well."

"What, we don't want a crowd of noisy brutes! Why should we take carts for them?"

"They will go on their own feet."

"Yes, and hinder us at every step, by stopping the cows to drink. Besides, the duke's chief reason for buying this herd, is, as I know, not to experiment with pure Hungarian cattle, but to cross them with his Spanish breed."

"Of course that is quite another thing," said the overseer.

There now remained nothing else to do but to start the new bought herd. The manager gave the herdsman his credentials, and the chief constable handed him his pass. These documents, together with the cattle certificates, he put into his bag. Then he tied the bell round the bull's neck, knotted his cloak round its horns, and bidding everyone good day, sprang into the saddle. The overseer brought him his knapsack, filled with bacon, bread, and garlic, enough for the week that they would take to reach Miskolcz. Then he described the whole route to him. How they must first go by Polgár, because of the mud at Csege, caused by the spring rains, and sleep on the way in the little wood. They would cross the Theiss by the ferry-boat, but should the water be high, it would be better to wait there, and give hay to the beasts rather than risk an accident.

Then he impressed on his godson the necessity of so behaving in a foreign country that Debreczin need never blush for him. "He must obey his employers, hold his high spirits in check, never forget Hungarian, nor abandon his faith, but keep all the Church feasts, and not squander his earnings. If he married he must take care of his wife, and give his children Hungarian names, and when he had time he might write a line to his godfather, who would willingly pay the postage."

Then, with a godfather's blessing, he left the young fellow to set out on his journey.

Now the two Moravian drovers had undertaken the task of driving the herd, when free from the enclosure, in the desired direction, but naturally the beasts, as soon as they were set at liberty, rushed about on all sides, and when the drovers attempted to force them, turned, and prepared to run at them. Then they again made for the corral and their calves.

"Go and help those poor Christians!" said the overseer to the herdsman.

"Better crack the whip among them," suggested the painter.

"The devil take your whip," growled the overseer; "do you want them to run to the four ends of the earth? These are no horses!"

"I said they ought to be tied together in pairs by their horns," cried the manager.

"All right, just leave it to me."

With that the cowherd whistled, and a little sheep-dog jumped from the karám, and barking loudly, scampered after the disordered herd, dashed round the scattered animals, snapped at the heels of the lazy ones, and in less than two minutes had brought the whole drove into a well-ordered military file, marching behind the bull with the bell.

Then the cowherd also bounded after them, crying "Hi, Rosa! Csáko! Kese!" He knew the name of everyone of the twenty-four, and they obeyed. As for the bull, it was called "Büszke" – "Proud one."

Thus, under this leadership, the herd moved quietly off over the wide plain. For long the gentlemen gazed after it, till it arrived at the brink of the quivering fairy sea. Then suddenly each beast grew gigantic, more like a mammoth than a cow, jet black in color, and with legs growing to a fearful length, until at last there appeared to be attached to them a second cow, moving along with the other, only upside down. Herdsmen, dog, drovers, all followed them head downwards.

The painter sank back on the grass, his arms and legs extended.

"Well, if I tell this at the Art Club in Vienna, they will kick me out at the door."

"A bad sign," said Mr. Sajgató, shaking his head. "It's well the money is in my pocket."

"Yes, the cattle are not home yet," muttered the overseer.

"What I wonder at," observed the manager, "is why some enterprising individual has not taken the whole show on lease."

"Ah!" said Mr. Sajgató with proud stolidity. "No doubt they would take it to Vienna if they could. But Debreczin won't give it up."

Chapter IV

The veterinary and his gig jolted merrily over the puszta. His good little horse knew its lesson by heart, and needed neither whip nor bridle. So, the doctor could take out his notebook, reckon, and scribble. All at once, looking up, he noticed a csikós approaching, his horse galloping wildly.

The pace was so mad that both rider and steed seemed to be out of their minds. Suddenly the horse rushed towards him, stood still, reared, and then swerved aside, taking another direction. Its rider sat with head thrown back, and arched body, clutching the bridle in both hands, while the horse shook itself, and began to neigh and snort in a frightened manner.

Seeing this, the doctor seized whip and reins, and made every endeavor to overtake the horseman. As he got closer he recognized the csikós. "Sándor Decsi!" he exclaimed. And the rider appeared to know him also, and to slacken the bridle as if to allow the horse to go nearer. The clever animal reached the doctor's gig, puffing and blowing, and there stopped of its own accord. It shook its head, snorted, and, in fact, did everything but speak.

The lad sat in the saddle, bent backwards, his face staring at the sky. The bridle had dropped from his fingers, but his legs still gripped the sides of his horse.

"Sándor, lad! Sándor Decsi!" called the doctor. But the boy seemed not to hear him, or hearing, to be incapable of speech.

Jumping from his trap, the doctor went up to the rider, caught him round the waist, and lifted him out of the saddle.

"What ails you?" he said.

But the lad was silent. His mouth was shut, his neck bent back, and his breath came in quick gasps. His eyes, wide open, had a ghastly gleam, which the dilation of the pupils rendered all the more hideous.

Laying him flat on the turf, the doctor began to examine him. "Pulse irregular, sometimes quick, sometimes stopping completely, pupils widely dilated, jaws tightly closed, back curved. This young fellow has been *poisoned!*" he cried, "and with some vegetable poison, too."

The doctor had found the csikós midway between the Hortobágy inn and the little settlement at Mata. Probably he was on his way to the hamlet when the poison first began to act, and had tried as long as consciousness lasted to get there; but when the spasms seized him, his movements became involuntary, and the convulsive twitching of his arms had startled the horse. It was also foaming at the mouth.

The doctor next attempted to lift him into the gig, but the lad was too heavy, and he could not manage it. Still, to leave him on the puszta was impossible. Before he could return with help the eagles would already be there, tearing at the unfortunate man. All this time the horse looked on intelligently, as if it would speak, and, now bending its head over its master, it gave some short abrupt snorts.

"Well, help me then," said the doctor.

Why should he not understand, a puszta steed, who has three-quarters of a soul at least? Seeing the doctor struggling with his master, it caught hold of his waistcoat with his teeth, and raised him, and so between them, they managed to get the csikós into the gig. Then the doctor knotted the horse's halter to the back of the trap, and galloped on to the settlement.

There, it is true, were hospital and pharmacy, but only for animals. The doctor himself was but a cattle doctor. In such cases, however, he may help who can. The question was, could he?

The first thing to do was to discover what poison was at work, strychnine or belladonna. At all events, black coffee could do no harm.

Arrived at the farm, the doctor called out his assistant and his housekeeper. Coffee was ready, but aid was necessary before the patient could swallow. His jaws were so tightly locked that they had to force his teeth apart with a chisel before it could be poured down.

"Ice on his head, a mustard plaster on his stomach," ordered the doctor; and there being no spare person at hand, he carried out his own directions, at the same time giving instructions to his assistant, and writing a letter at the table. "Listen," he said, "and think of what I am telling you. Hurry in the gig to the Hortobágy inn, and hand this letter to the innkeeper. If he is not at home, then tell the coachman my orders are to put the horses in the caléche, and go as fast as he possibly can to town, and give this sealed letter to the head doctor there. He must wait and bring him back. I am a veterinary surgeon, and on oath not to practice on beasts 'with souls.' The case needs help urgently, and the doctor will bring his own medicine. But ask the innkeeper's daughter for every grain of coffee she may have in the house, for that the patient must drink until the real doctor comes. Now, see how sharp you can be!"

The assistant understood the task imposed on him, and made all haste to get under way. The poor little grey had hardly had breathing time before it was rattling back to the inn.

Klári happened to be on the verandah, watering her musk-geraniums, when the gig drove up.

"What brings you, Pesta," she asked, "in such a fearful hurry?"

"A letter for the master."

"Well, it will be difficult to get a word out of him, because he is just putting a new swarm into the hive."

"But it is an order from the vet," said Pesta, "to send the carriage to town immediately for the best doctor."

"The doctor? Is someone ill? Who has the ague now?"

"None of us, for the doctor picked him up on the meadow. It is Sándor Decsi, the csikós."

The girl gave a cry, and the watering-can fell from her hands. "Sándor? Sándor is ill?"

"So ill that he is trying to climb up the wall, and bite the bed-clothes in his agony. Somebody has poisoned him."

The girl had to clutch the door with both hands to prevent herself falling.

"Our doctor is not sure what is killing the herdsman, so he is obliged to summon the town doctor to inspect him."

Then Klári muttered something, but what could not be heard.

"See, leave go the door, miss," said the assistant, "and let me in to look for the master."

"Doesn't he know what has hurt him?" stammered the girl.

"And the doctor's message to you," added Pesta, "is to collect all the ground coffee in the house, and give it to me. Till the other doctor comes with medicine, he is treating Sándor Decsi with coffee, for he can't tell what poison they gave the poor fellow." Then he hurried off to search for the innkeeper.

"He can't tell what poison," murmured Klári to herself, "but I can – if that be the danger, why I could tell the doctor, and then he would at once know what to give him."

She ran into her room, and opening the chest took from its bottom, the man-shaped witch roots. These she stuffed into her pocket.

Cursed be she who had given the evil counsel, and cursed be she who had followed it!

Then she set to work grinding coffee, so that by the time the assistant returned from the garden, where he had been forced to help with the swarm, the tin box was quite full.

"Now give me the coffee, miss," said he.

"I am coming with you."

The assistant was a sharp lad and saw through the sieve. "Do not come, miss," he said, "you really must not see Sándor Decsi in such a state. It is enough to freeze one's marrow to look at his agony. Besides, the doctor would never allow it."

"It is just the doctor I want to speak to," said the girl.

"But then who will attend to the customers?"

"The servant-girl is here, and the lad, they'll manage."

"But at least ask the master's permission," begged Pesta.

"Not I!" cried Klári, "he would not let me go. There, get out of the way."

So saying, she pushed the assistant aside, flew out into the courtyard, and with one bound was seated in the gig. There she seized the reins, flourished the whip about the poor grey's back, and drove where she wished. The assistant left behind gasping, shouted after her,

"Miss Klári! Miss Klári! Stop a bit!" But though he ran till he was breathless, he only caught the gig at the bridge, where the tired horse had to go slowly up the incline. Then he too jumped on to the seat.

Never had the grey's back felt such thwacks as on this drive to Mata! By the time they reached the sandy ground, it could only go at a walk, and, the girl, impatient, sprang from the gig, and catching hold of the canister, rushed over the clover field to the doctor's farm, which she reached panting and speechless.

Through the window the doctor saw her coming and went to meet her, barring her way at the verandah.

"You come here, Klárika! How is that?"

"Sándor?" gasped the girl.

"Sándor is ill."

Through the open door the girl could hear the groans of the sick man.

"What has happened to him?"

"I don't know myself, and I don't want to accuse anyone."

"But I know!" cried the girl, "someone – a wicked girl – gave him something bad to drink. I know who it was too! She stirred it into his wine, to make him love her, and that made him ill. I know who it was, and how it was."

"Miss Klári, do not play the traitor. This is a serious crime, and must be proved."

"Here are the proofs."

And with that girl took the roots out of her pocket, and laid them before the doctor.

"Oh!" cried the doctor, stupefied, "why, this is *Atropa mandragora* – a deadly poison!"

The girl clapped her hands to her face, "How did I know it was poison?" she asked.

"Klárika," said the doctor, "do not startle me more or I shall jump out of the window. Surely *you* did not poison Sándor?"

The girl nodded mutely.

"And what in thunder did you do it for?"

"He was so unkind to me, and once a gypsy woman made me believe that if I steeped that root in his wine I should have him at my feet again."

"Well, I never. . . ! You must hold traffic with gypsy women, must you? To school you won't go, where the master would teach you to distinguish poisonous plants. No, no, you will only learn from a gypsy vagabond! Well, you have made your lad nice and obedient!"

"Will he die?" asked the girl with an imploring look.

"Die? Must he die next? No, his body and soul are not stitched together in such a ramshackle fashion."

"Then he will live!" cried the girl, and knelt down before the doctor, snatching his hands, and kissing them repeatedly.

"Don't kiss my hand," said he, "it is all over mustard plaster, and will make your mouth swell."

So she kissed his feet, and when he forbade that, also his footprints. Down on the brick floor she went and kissed the muddy footprints with her pretty, rosy lips.

"Now, stand up and talk sense," said the doctor. "Have you brought the coffee? ground and roasted? Right – for that is what he must drink till the doctor comes. It is well you told me what poison the lad took, for now I know the antidote. But as for you, child, make up your mind to vanish from these parts as soon as you like, for what you have done is a crime, which the town doctor will report, and the matter will come before the court and judge. So fly away, where there are no tongues to tell on you."

"I won't fly," said the girl, drying her tears with her apron. "Here is my neck, more I can't offer. If I have done wrong, it is only just that I should suffer for it, but from this spot I won't stir! The groaning I hear through the door binds me faster than if my feet were in fetters. Doctor! sir! for God's sake let me be near to nurse him, to foment his head, smooth his pillows, and wipe the sweat from his brow."

"Indeed! Is that your idea? Why, they would clap me into the madhouse, if I entrusted the nursing of the victim to the poisoner."

A look of unspeakable pain came over the girl's face.

"Does the doctor believe that I am really bad then?" she asked. Glancing round she caught sight of the damnatory root lying on the windowsill, and before he could stop her, had grasped it, and was putting it into her mouth.

"No, no, Klárika," said the doctor, "do not play with that poison. Don't bite it, take it out of your mouth instantly. I would rather allow you to go to the patient, though it is no sight for you, as I tell you beforehand. No tender-hearted person should see such suffering."

"I know; your assistant told me everything. How one cannot recognize him, his face is so changed. Dark blotches instead of healthy red color, deathlike shadow on his forehead, and cold perspiration shining on his cheeks. His eyes are wide open with a glassy stare, his lips seem gummed together, and if he opens them they foam. How he groans, struggles, gnashes his teeth, tosses his arms about, and contorts his back! An agonizing sight! But let this be my punishment, to feel his moans and sufferings, like so many sharp knives stabbing my heart. And if I do not actually witness them with my own eyes and ears, I shall still seem to see and hear them as acutely as if I was really present."

"Well," said the doctor, "let us see if you are really brave enough. Take charge of the coffee-pot, and have black coffee always ready; but if you burst out crying I will push you out of the room."

Then he opened the door and allowed her to enter.

The world went blue and green to the girl as her eyes fell on her sweetheart lying there. Where was the radiant young fellow who had left her such a short time ago? Now it was painful to look at him, to endure the sight of him.

The doctor called in his assistant, and the girl stifled her sobs as best she might, over the coffee-pot. If the doctor caught the sound of one he would glance at her reproachfully, and she would pretend it was a cough.

The two men applied mustard plasters to the patient's feet.

"Now bring your coffee and pour it into his mouth," said the doctor.

But that was a business! Both had to exert their full strength to hold down the lad's arms, and prevent his flinging them about.

"Now, Klárika, open his mouth; not like that! You must force his teeth apart with the chisel. Don't be afraid, he won't swallow it. See, he holds it as fast as a vice."

The girl obeyed.

"Now pour in the coffee by the spout, gently. There you are a clever girl. I can recommend you to the Sisters of Mercy as a sick nurse!"

There was a smile on the girl's face, but her heart was breaking.

"If only he would not look at me with those eyes!"

"Yes," said the doctor, "that is the worst of all, those two staring eyes. I think so too."

At length there seemed some little improvement, possibly the effect of the remedy. The patient's groans became less frequent, and the cramp in his limbs relaxed, but his forehead burned like fire. The doctor instructed the girl how to wring out the cold water bandage – lay it on the aching head, leave it a little, and then change it again. She did all that he bade her.

"Now I see that you have a brave heart," he said, and in time came her reward, for to her joy the sufferer suddenly closed his eyelids, and the terrible stare of those black-shadowed eyes ceased altogether. Later his mouth relaxed and they were able to open the close-shut jaws without difficulty.

Maybe it was the prompt application of the antidote; maybe the dose of poison had not been strong, but by the time the doctor from town had arrived, the patient was very unmistakably better. The veterinary and the doctor conversed in Latin, which the girl could not understand, but her instinct told her that it was of her they were speaking. Then the doctor ordered this and that, and after writing the *usum repertum,* returned to his carriage, and hastened back to town.

Not so the gendarme whom he had brought with him on the box. He remained. Hardly had the physician gone, when another trap rumbled into the yard. This was the Hortobágy innkeeper, who had come to demand his daughter.

"Gently now, master," they said, "the young woman is under arrest. Don't you see the gendarme?"

"I always did say that when once a girl loses her head she goes mad altogether. Well, it's no concern of mine." And with charming indifference the old innkeeper thereupon turned and drove back to the Hortobágy inn.

Chapter V

All night long the girl watched beside him – to no one would she yield her place at the sick bed. She had been up till dawn the night before as well, but how differently occupied! This was her penance.

Now and then she nodded sleepily in her chair, but the slightest moan from the sick man sufficed to wake her. Sometimes she renewed the cold bandage on his head, and bathed her own eyes to keep herself awake. At the first cock-crow kindly sleep settled softly on the patient. He stretched himself out and began to snore with beautiful regularity. At first the girl was terrified, and thought the death struggle was at hand, but presently she grew very happy. This was a good honest snore, such as could only emanate from healthy lungs; and besides, as she reflected, it kept her wide awake. When the cock crew for the second time, he was in a sound slumber.

Then he started from sleep and yawned widely.

Thank heaven! He could yawn again.

The spasms had quite ceased, and all who suffer from their nerves know the worth of a good yawn after the attack. It is as good as a lottery prize.

The girl wished to give him more coffee, but the man shook his head. "Water," he murmured.

So she rapped through to the doctor, who was reposing in the next room, to know if she might give the patient water, as he was asking for it.

The doctor rose, and came out in dressing gown and slippers, to see for himself. He was most satisfied. "He is going on well; to be thirsty is a good sign. Give him as much water as he wants." The invalid drank a whole carafe and then dropped into a quiet slumber.

"Now he is fast asleep," said the doctor to Klári, "so you may go and lie down on the bed in the housekeeper's room. I will leave my door open, and take care of him."

But the girl pleaded so hard to be allowed to stay, to lean her head on the table and thus steal a nap, that he at last let her do as she pleased. Suddenly she awoke with a start to find it was day, and the sparrows were twittering at the windows.

The patient was then dreaming as well as sleeping. His lips moved, he murmured something and laughed. His eyes half opened, but evidently with a great effort, for they closed immediately. But his parched lips seemed to be asking for something.

"Shall I give you water?" whispered the girl.

"Yes," he muttered, with his eyes shut.

So she brought him the water bottle, but he had not strength enough in his arms – this great fellow – even to raise the tumbler to his mouth. She had to lift his head and give it to him. Even while drinking he fell half asleep.

Hardly had his head touched the pillow when he began to hum aloud – probably a continuation of the gay air of his dreams:

"Why not love this world of ours?

Gypsy maid, Magyar maid, both are flowers."

Chapter VI

A day or two later the lad was on his feet again. Such tough fellows as he, born and bred on the puszta, do not linger long on the sick list when once the crisis is past. They abhor bed. So on the third day he told the doctor that he wished to get back to the horses at his place of service.

"Wait a bit, Sándor, my boy. Somebody has to speak with you first."

"Somebody" turned out to be the examining magistrate. On the third day, after the report, this official, with his notary and a gendarme, arrived at Mata to conduct the formal inquiry. The accused – the young woman – had already been examined, and had given a full account of everything. She denied nothing, only saying in her defense that she was very much in love with Sándor, and wished to make him love her as well.

All this was taken down in the protocol and signed. Nothing now remained but to confront the prisoner with her victim. And this was done as soon as the herdsman had regained sufficient strength.

Meanwhile he never once uttered the girl's name in the doctor's presence, pretending not to know that she had been in the house nursing him, and as the young man recovered consciousness, she ceased to show herself at all. Before confronting her with him, the magistrate read out the deposition to the girl, who confirmed it anew, and would not have a word altered.

Then Sándor Decsi was brought forward.

As soon as the csikós entered the room he began to act a preconcerted rôle. His swaggering betyár airs were such that one would have thought he had only learnt to play the csikós on the stage. When the judge asked his name he stared at him over his shoulder.

"My worthy name? Sándor Decsi! I have hurt no one, nor have I stolen anything, that I should be dragged here by gendarmes. Besides, I am not under civil authority. I am still a soldier of the Emperor, and if anyone has a complaint against me, let him go before the regimental authorities, and there I will answer him."

The magistrate silenced him. "Gently, young man, no one is accusing you of anything. We only want enlightenment in an affair closely concerning yourself. That is the object of this investigation. Tell us when were you last in the taproom of the Hortobágy inn?"

"I can inform you exactly. What is there to hide? But first send away this gendarme at my back. Because if he should happen to come too near, I am touchy and might give him a blow."

"Now, now, not so fast, young fellow. The gendarme is not guarding you. Tell us when it was that you visited Miss Klári here – the day she served you with wine?"

"Well, I will as soon as I have got my wits together. The last time I was at the Hortobágy inn was last year, on Demeter's day, when they engage the shepherds.

Then they took me for a soldier, and I have not been in the place since."

"Sándor!" broke in the girl.

"Yes, Sándor is my name. So they christened me."

"Then you were not there three days ago, when the barmaid gave you the wine mixed with mandragora, which made you so ill?"

"I *never* was at the Hortobágy inn, nor did I see Miss Klári. It is half a year since I asked for any of her wine!"

"Sándor, you are lying for my sake!" cried the girl.

The judge grew angry.

"Do not try to mislead the authorities with your denials. The girl has already confessed everything – that she made you drink wine poisoned with mandrake roots."

"Why, then, the young woman lied," said the herdsman.

"But what reason could she have for accusing herself of a crime which entails such heavy punishment?"

"Why, what reason? Because when the mad fit comes upon a girl, she simply raves without rhyme or reason. Miss Klári fancies our eyes don't meet each other's often enough, so she has an ill will against me, and now she takes to accusing herself to compel me to let out the *other one's* name, out of sheer compassion – the pretty lass, to whom I went to lose my soul and cure my heart, and who gave me the charm to drink. Well, if I choose I'll tell, but if I don't, I won't. This is Miss Klári's revenge for my having neither called on her, nor gone near her since I came home on leave."

At these words the girl turned on him like a fury.

"Sándor! – you who have never lied in your life – what ails you? When the one little lie, which they put in your mouth, would have saved you from soldiering, that you could not tell! Now you deny being with me three days ago. Then who brought me the comb that I have done up my hair with?"

The csikós laughed grimly.

"Who brought it, and why? Surely the young lady knows better than I!"

"Sándor, this is not right of you! I don't mind if they put me in the pillory for my wrong-doing, and lash and scourge me. Here is my head; let them cut it off if they like. But don't tell me you never cared for me, nor came to see me, for that is worse than death."

The judge flew into a rage. "Confound you," he cried. "Settle your love affairs between yourselves. Since a flagrant case of poisoning has been committed, I want to know who was the culprit!"

"Now answer!" exclaimed the girl, with flaming cheeks. "Answer that!"

"Well, well. Since I must, so be it, I can tell you all about it. On the Ohát puszta I fell in with a gypsy band in tents. One of them, a lovely girl, with eyes like sloes, who was standing outside, spoke to me, and invited me in. They were roasting a sucking pig, and we enjoyed ourselves. I drank their wine, and at once felt that it had a bitter taste; but the kisses of the gypsy lass were so sweet that I forgot all about it."

"You *lie, lie, lie!*" shrieked the girl. "You have invented that story this very minute!"

The herdsman laughed loudly, clapped one hand to the crown of his head, snapped his fingers in the air, and started his favorite song:

"Why not love this world of ours?
Gypsy maid, Magyar maid, both are flowers."

Not this very minute had he invented this tale, but on that night of pain when the "Yellow Rose" had sat smoothing his pillows and bathing his brow. Then, with his aching head, he had thought out a plan to save his faithless sweetheart.

The judge struck his fist on the table.

"None of your nonsense before me, making fun of the matter."

"I make fun of the matter!" exclaimed the csikós, becoming serious instantly. "I swear before God above, all I have said is true."

He raised his three fingers, and the girl screamed out,

"No, no! Do not perjure yourself! Do not risk the salvation of your soul!"

"The devil take you both, for you are both mad." This was the judge's verdict. "Notary, take down the herdsman's statement regarding the gypsy, who will be charged with committing the crime. As to her whereabouts, that the police must discover. It is their business. You two can go; if necessary, we will summon you again."

Then they let the girl free. She deserved a little fatherly rebuke, and that she got.

The lad remained behind to hear his deposition taken down, and to sign it. The girl waited on the verandah for him to come out, his horse being tethered to an acacia hard by.

The lad, however, first went to the doctor to thank him for his unremitting kindness. The doctor having attended the inquiry, had, of course, heard everything.

"Well, Sándor," he said, as soon as the thanks had been got over, "I have seen many famous actors on the stage, but never one who played the betyár as you did!"

"I did right, didn't I?" asked the lad gravely.

"Yes, indeed, you are an honorable fellow. But say a kind word to the girl if you meet her. Poor thing, she never meant to do such wrong."

"I am not angry with her. May God bless you, sir, for your great goodness."

As he stepped out on to the verandah, the girl stopped him, and seized his hand.

"Sándor, what have you done? Sent your soul to perdition, sworn falsely, told a lying tale, all to set me free! You have denied ever having loved me, that my body may escape the lash, and my slender neck the blow that would sever it. Why have you done this?"

"That is my affair. This much I will tell you; from henceforth, one of us two I must hate and despise. Do not cry, you are not that one! I dare no longer look in your eyes, because I see myself reflected there, and I am worth no more than the broken button that is coming off my waistcoat. God bless you."

With that he untied his horse from the acacia, sprang on to it, and dashed off into the puszta.

The girl gazed and gazed after him, till her sight grew dim from tears. Then she sought till she found the broken button he had cast on the floor. This she placed next her heart.

Chapter VII

It happened just as the overseer had predicted. When the herd reached the Polgár ferry it was impossible to cross. The Theiss, the Sajó, the Hernád, all were in flood. The water touched the planking of the foot-bridge. The ferry-boat had been hauled up, and moored to the willows on the bank. Great trees, torn up by their roots, were coming down on the turbulent dirty flood; and flocks of wild ducks, divers, and cormorants were disporting themselves on the waters, fearless of the gun at such a time.

But that communication should be stopped was a dire misfortune, not only for the Duke's cattle, but much more so for all the market-goers from Debreczin and Újváros, striving to reach the Onod fair. There stood their carts, out among the puddles, under the open sky, while their owners bewailed the bad luck in the one small drinking-room of the Polgár ferry-house.

Ferko Lacza went off to buy hay for the herd, and purchased a whole stack. "For here we can sit kicking our heels for three days at the shortest!"

Now, by good luck, there was, among those bound for the market, a purveyor of cooked meat, with her enormous iron frying pan, and fresh pork, ready sliced.

She found a ready sale for her wares, setting up a makeshift cook-shop in a hut constructed of maize stalks. Firewood she did not need to buy, the Theiss brought plenty. Wine the old innkeeper had, sharp, but good, since none better was to be got. Besides, every Hungarian carries his pipe, tobacco, and his bag of provisions when he gives his mind to travel.

So the time passed in forming new acquaintances. The Debreczin bootmaker and the tanner from Balmaz-Újváros were old friends, while the vendor of cloaks was universally addressed as "Daddy." The ginger-bread baker, who thought himself better than the others because he wore a long coat with a scarlet collar, sat at a separate table, but, nevertheless, joined in the conversation. Later, a horse-cooper appeared; but as his nose was crooked, he was only allowed to talk standing. When the cowherd entered, a place was squeezed out for him at the table, for even townsfolk respect a herdsman's position of trust. The Moravian drovers stayed outside to watch the cattle.

The tittle-tattle went on pleasantly and quietly as yet, young Mistress Pundor not having arrived. When she put in an appearance, nobody would get in a word edgeways. But her cart had evidently stuck on the way, at some seductive inn, she having seized the opportunity of traveling with the carpenter, her brother-in-law. He was taking tulip-decorated chests to the Onod fair, while young Mistress Pundor supplied the world with soap and tallow candles. When the herdsman entered, the room was so full of smoke that he could hardly see.

"Then tell us, 'Daddy,'" the shoemaker was saying to the tanner, "for you at Újváros are nearer the Hortobágy inn than we; how did the innkeeper's girl poison the csikós?"

At these words the cowboy felt as if he had been shot through the heart.

"How was it? Well, pretty little Klárika there peppered the stew she was making him with crows' claws."

"I know otherwise," interrupted the ginger-bread baker. "Little Klári put datura in the honeymead – the stuff they use for stupefying fish."

"Well, of course, the gentleman must know best, for he has a gold watch chain! They sent for the regimental surgeon from Újváros to dissect the deceased csikós, and he found the claws in his inside. They put them in spirits, to be produced as evidence at the trial!"

"So you have killed the poor fellow! We didn't hear he died from the poison, only went mad, and was sent up to Buda to have a hole bored in his head, for all the strength of the poison had gone there."

"Sent him up to Buda, did they? Sent him underground, you mean! Why, my wife herself spoke to the very maker of imitation flowers who made those strewn over Decsi's shroud. That is a fact!"

"Now, now! Mistress Csikmak is here with her fried meat, and as she came a day later from Debreczin, she must know the truth. Let us call her in."

But Mistress Csikmak, being unable to leave her frizzling pan, could only give her opinion through the window. She, likewise, buried the poisoned csikós. The Debreczin clerk had chanted over his grave, and the priest had preached a farewell sermon.

"And what happened to the girl?" inquired three voices at once.

"The girl! She ran off with her lover – a cowboy; by whose advice she poisoned the csikós. They are setting up a robber band together."

Ferko Lacza listened quietly to all this.

"Stuff and nonsense. Bosh!" exclaimed the gingerbread baker, capping her version. "I'm afraid you've not heard right, dear Mistress Csikmak. They caught the girl directly, put her in irons, and brought her in between gendarmes. My lad was there when they took her to the Town-House."

Still the cowherd listened without stirring.

Suddenly, amid great commotion, arrived the above-mentioned laggard – young Mistress Pundor, she foremost, then the driver, lastly the brother-in-law, dragging a large chest. How polite a language is Hungarian, even an individual like the soap-making lady has her title of respect, "ifjasszony" (young mistress).

"Now Mistress Pundor will tell us what happened to the girl at the inn who poisoned the csikós," cried everyone.

"Yes, of course. Dear soul. Just let me get my breath a bit." With that she sat down on the large chest, a chair or bench would have smashed to atoms under her form.

"Did they catch pretty Klári? or has she run away?"

"Oh, my dears, why they have tried her already, condemned to death she is, tomorrow they put her in the convict's cell, and the execution is the day after. The headsman comes today from Szeged, and they have taken a room for him at the White Horse, because the folks at the Bull refused him. 'Tis as true as I'm sitting here. I have it from the porter himself, who comes to me for candles."

"And what sort of death is she to have?"

"Well, under the old rule – and richly she deserves it – they would set her on straw and burn her. But seeing she is of the better class, and her father of good family, they will only cut off her head. They generally behead gentlefolk."

"Ah, quit that, mistress," contradicted the gingerbread man. "Do they heed such things nowadays? Not a bit of it! Why, before '48, if I put on my mantle with the silver buttons, they took me for – a gentleman, and never asked me for toll on the bridge at Pest, but now I may wear my mantle –"

"Oh, drop your mantle with the silver buttons!" said the cloth merchant, taking the word out of his mouth.

"Let the young mistress here tell us what she has heard. What object could the pretty lass have for contriving such a murder?"

"Ah, 'tis a very strange business. One murder leads to another. A while ago, a rich Moravian cattle-dealer came here buying cattle. He had much money. Pretty Klári, there, talked it over with her lover, the cowherd, and together they murdered the dealer, and threw him into the Hortobágy. But the horseherd, who was also sweet on the girl, caught them at it, and so first they divided the stolen money between them, and then poisoned the csikós to put him out of the way."

"And what about the cowherd then, has he been caught?" inquired the bootmaker excitedly.

"They would if they could, but he has vanished utterly. Gendarmes are searching the whole puszta for him, and a price is set on his head. They have stuck up his description, as I have read for myself, a hundred dollars to whoever catches him alive. I know him well enough too!"

Now, had Sándor Decsi been sitting there instead of Ferko Lacza, great would have been the scene, for here was the moment for a real effective bit of drama. To fling his loaded cudgel on the table, knock the chair from under him, and shout out, "I am the herdsman on whose head they have set a price. Which of you wants the hundred dollars?"

Then the whole worthy company would have taken to their heels and fled, some to the cellar, some up the chimney.

But the cowboy was of a different temperament, and had been used all his life to act with care and caution. Besides, his work among the cattle had impressed upon him the imprudence of catching the bull by the horns.

So leaning his elbows on the table, he asked calmly, "Would you then recognize the herdsman from the description, mistress?"

"Why not indeed! How could I help knowing him? He has bought my soap often enough to be sure!"

"But, dear me, ma'am," said the horse-cooper, who desired to display his knowledge, "what use can a herdsman have for soap? Surely, all cowboys wear blue shirts and breeches which never need washing, because the linen has been first boiled in lard!"

"Deary me! Sakes alive! Did you ever! So soap is only wanted for dirty clothes, is it? A cowboy never shaves, does he? Perhaps he always wears as long a beard as a Jew horse-cooper?"

Everyone shrieked with laughter, much to the discomfiture of the snubbed intruder.

"Now, need I have exposed myself to that?" grumbled the unhappy man.

"You don't happen to know the name," continued the herdsman, in a quiet voice, "of that cowboy, mistress?"

"Not know his name! It has but just slipped out of my mind. 'Tis on the tip of my tongue, for I know him as well as my own child."

"Is it Ferko Lacza?"

"Yes, yes, that's it. Why, you've taken it out of my mouth. Perhaps you know him yourself?"

But the herdsman refrained from announcing that he knew him as well as his father's only son. Quietly knocking out the ashes from his pipe, he refilled it, rose, and propped up his cudgel against the straw-bottomed chair to show it was engaged, and no one else might occupy it. Then, relighting his pipe at the solitary candle burning on the middle of the table, he left the room. Those remaining made remarks about him.

"Surely something heavy as lead is weighing on that man!"

"I don't like the look of his eyes!"

"Could he know aught about the csikós' murder, think you?"

Again the horse-dealer committed the offence of meddling in the discussion.

"Ladies and gentlemen," he said, "permit me to make the humble observation that yesterday, when I was on the Ohát puszta, buying horses, I there saw the murdered and poisoned Sándor Decsi, looking as fresh and blooming as a rosy apple! He lassoed the colts for me. This is as true as I live!"

"*What?* And you let us sit here telling lies to one another?" stormed the whole assembly. "Here, clear out; get away!"

No sooner said than done, they seized him by the collar and flung him out of the room.

The chucked-out traveler, smoothing his crumpled hat, spluttered and swore, till he found a moral to fit the case.

"Now, need I have exposed myself to that? What is the good of a Jew speaking the truth?"

Meanwhile, the cowherd going to the cattle proposed to the Moravian drovers that they should go inside for a change and drink a glass of wine; he would watch the cows. The chair with the stick beside it was his.

While he watched he picked up a bit of "poor man's peat," stuffing it up his coat sleeve. What could he want with it?

Chapter VIII

Lucky it is that no one outside the Hortobágy knows about this "poor man's peat" which is gathered on the meadow-land. One thing is certain – it is no lily-of-the-valley. It is the sole fuel of the puszta herdsman, in fact, a sort of zoological peat.

We remember the tale of the Hungarian landowner who, finding it advisable to go abroad after the Revolution, chose free Switzerland as a temporary place of residence. But his eyes never grew used to the high mountains. Every evening, on withdrawing to his room, he would take a piece of "peat," found on the pasture, and laying it on the hearth, kindle it. Then, as he sat with closed eyes in the smell of the smoke, he would once more fancy himself back on the wide, wide plains, among the moving herds and tinkling cow bells, and all the rest for which his soul longed. . . .

Well, if this peat-smoke can exert such a strong influence on an educated mind, how were it possible to doubt the following story?

The travelers had to wait two more days at the Polgár ferry.

On the third, about midnight, the ferry-man brought the glad tidings to the expectant crowd, whose patience and provisions were alike exhausted, that the Theiss had fallen greatly. The ferry-boat had been replaced, and by morning they would be able to cross.

Those with carts lost no time in running them on board, and arranging them side by side. Next they took the horses. Then came the turn for the cattle. Room was made for them with difficulty. The crush was great, but mild, after all, to what theater-goers usually endure!

Last of all, the bull, the terror of everyone, was brought, and now no one remained but the herdsman and his horse. The two Moravian drovers took their places between the cows and the carts. But as yet no start could be made. The tow-rope was strained taut by the water, and they were obliged to wait till the sunshine could relax it somewhat. Moisture was rising like steam all along its surface.

So the cowherd, wishing to utilise the time, suggested that the ferry-man might cook them a "paprikás" of fish. Nothing else eatable was to be had, but a pot was at hand, likewise plenty of fish, left by the receding waters. The boatmen caught them by sticking an oar under their gills – fat carp, silurius, and sturgeon. These they hastily cleaned, cut up, and cast into the pot, underneath which a little fire was kindled.

Now all was ready, when the question rose: "Who has 'paprika'?" Every ordinary, self-respecting Hungarian carries his own supply in his knapsack; but after a three days' famine even "paprika" will give out! Nevertheless, no "paprika," no fish stew.

"I have some," said the cowboy, and pulled a wooden box from his sleeve. Everyone noted what a far-seeing man he must be to reserve his own "paprika" for the last extremity, and henceforth regarded him as the saviour of the party.

The stew-pot was in the end of the ferry-boat, and to reach it the herdsman traversed its whole length, the cattle being stationed about the middle. But, then, who cares to let his box of "paprika" out of his own hand? While the ferry-man was busy seasoning the fish with the red pepper (Oken, writing about it, calls it *poison*; but that some wild tribes dare to eat it), the cowboy took the opportunity to drop his piece of "peat," unobserved into the fire.

"I say! that 'paprikás' must be singeing! What a smell it has!" remarked the cobbler presently.

"Smell! Stink I would call it," corrected the itinerant cloak vendor.

But the heavy greasy odor affected the noses of the cattle more markedly. First, the bull grew restless, snuffed in the air, shook the bell at his neck and lowed, then lowering his head and lifting his tail began to bellow dangerously. At that the cows got excited, capered to and fro, reared up on each others backs, and jostled to the side of the ferry-boat.

"Mother Mary! Holy Anna! Protect the ship!" shrieked the fat soap-maker.

"Hurry up, mistress! seat yourself opposite. That will steady her again," joked the shoemaker.

But it was no joke. Every man on board had to clutch the rope to keep the ferry-boat from tilting over; the other side dipped nearly to the water.

Suddenly the bull gave a bellow, and with one great bound, jumped into the river. Another moment, and everyone of the four and twenty cows had followed him over the edge.

The ferry was just about halfway across.

"Turn back! Turn back!" screamed the Moravian drovers, as the cattle swam straight towards the bank they had left. They wanted the ferry-boat to return instantly, that they might go after their beasts.

"The devil a bit of turning back!" shrieked the market folk. "We must cross! We are late enough for the fair as it is!"

"No need to howl, lads," said the herdsman, with exceeding calm. "I'll bring them to their right minds."

He jumped on his horse, led it along to the end of the ferry, and sticking spurs into its sides, leapt over the rail into the water.

"See, the cowherd will overtake them, no fear!" So the cobbler assured the despairing drovers.

But the horse-cooper, left behind on the bank, for he had not managed to find room for his horses on board, nor had wished to frighten them among so many cattle, was of a contrary opinion.

"You'll never see more of that herd!" he yelled to the travelers on the ferry-boat. "You may whistle for them!"

"There goes that Jonah again! Where is there a ham bone to shoot him with?" stormed the cobbler.

The herd neared the bank in straggling order, and reaching the shallows, waded out to dry land. The herdsman was behind, for cattle swim faster than a horse. When he too landed, he undid the stock-whip from his neck and cracked it loudly.

"There! He's turning them!" said the market people to console the drovers.

But the cracking of a whip only serves to make cattle run on the faster.

The passengers found much exercise for their wit in this cattle incident. The ferry-men assured them with oaths that it was not the first time by any means that it had happened. Beasts brought from the Hortobágy so often were assailed by home sickness that no sooner was the ferry-boat put in motion than they would turn restive and spring overboard, swim to the bank, and run back to the puszta.

"Men have the same love of home and country," said the ginger-bread man, who, having often read of it in books, recognized the complaint.

"Ah, yes!" exclaimed Mistress Pundor, "no doubt the cows have gone home to their little calves. That was the mistake, to separate the children from their dear mothers!"

"Now my idea is different," said the cobbler, who was nothing if not skeptical. "I have heard often enough that those cunning betyárs, when they want to scatter a herd, put some grease in their pipes. The beasts, when they smell it, go stark, staring mad, and scuttle away in all directions. Then it is easy enough for the betyár to catch a nice little lot for himself. Now I scent something of the sort in this business."

"What you smell something, Daddy, and you don't run away from it?"

Everyone laughed.

"Wait a bit! Just you wait till we get on shore!" said the cobbler.

The Moravian drovers, however, saw nothing laughable in the vagaries of their herd, nor even matter suitable for a discussion on natural history, but began howling and lamenting like burned-out gypsies.

The old ferry-man, who talked Slav, attempted to console them. "Now don't howl, lads. 'Nye stekat.' He's not stolen your cows, the good herdsman. Those two letters, 'D.T.,' on the copper plate at the side of his cap don't mean 'dastard, thief,' but Debreczin Town. He can't run off with them. When we come over again they'll all be standing there in a group. He'll drive them back, sure enough. Why even his dog went after him! But when we take the cattle on board again we must fasten the cows three together, and tie the bull by the horns to that iron ring. It will be all right, only you must pay the passage money twice."

A good hour and a half elapsed before the ferry-boat reached the other bank, unloaded, reloaded, and returned to the Hortobágy side of the river. Then the drovers ran up the hill to the ferry-house, and sought their cattle everywhere. But none were to be seen.

The horse-dealer said that the angry beasts had galloped madly past towards the brushwood, and had quickly disappeared among the willows. They did not go towards the high road, but ran down wind, heads to the ground, tails up, like beasts attacked by a plague of flies.

A belated potter, coming up from Újváros with a crockery-laden cart, related how somewhere on the puszta he had met with a herd of cattle, which with a horseman and dog at their heels, had dashed roaring along, towards the Zám hills. Coming to the Hortobágy river, they had all jumped in, and he had lost sight of both rider and cows among the thick reeds.

The ferry-man turned to the gaping drovers,

"Now you *may* howl, countrymen!" he said.

Chapter IX

The Ohát puszta is the pasture ground of the "mixed" stud. From the corral in the center, all round to the wide circle of horizon, nothing can be seen but horses grazing. Horses of all colors, which only the richness of the Hungarian language can find names for: bay, grey, black, white-faced, piebald, dappled, chestnut, flea-bitten, strawberry, skewbald, roan, cream-colored, and, what is rarest among foals, milk-white. Well does this variety of shade and color deserve to be called the "mixed" herd. A gentleman's stud is something very different, there only horses of one breed and coloring are to be found.

All the horse owners in Debreczin turn out their mares here, where, summer or winter, they never see a stable, and only the head csikós keeps account of their yearly increase. Here, too, the famous pacers are raised, which are sought for from afar; for not every horse can stand a sandy country, a mountain-bred one, for example, collapses if it once treads an Alföld road.

Scattered groups are to be seen grazing industriously round the stallions. For the horse is always feeding. Learned men say that when Jupiter created Minerva, he cast this curse on the horse, that it might always eat, yet never be filled.

Four or five mounted csikós watch over the herd, with its thousand or so unruly colts, and use their thick stock-whips to drive back the more adventurous.

The arrangement here is the same as with the cattle herd, the "karám" or shanty, kitchen, wind shelter and well. Only, there is neither barrow-boy, nor "poor man's peat," nor protecting watchdog, for the horse cannot endure any of the canine tribe, and whether it be dog or wolf, both get kicked.

Noon was approaching, and the widely scattered troops of horses began to draw towards the great well. Two carriages were also nearing from the direction of the Hortobágy bridge. The head csikós, a thickset, bony old man, shading his eyes with his hand, recognized the newcomers from afar – by their horses.

"One is Mr. Mihály Kádár, the other, Pelikan, the horse-dealer. I knew, when I looked in my calendar, that they would honor me to day."

"Then, is that written in the calendar?" asked Sándor, the herdsman, surprised.

"Yes, my boy! Everything is in 'Csathy's Almanack.' The Onod cattle market is on Sunday, and Pelikan must take horses there."

His prognostications were correct. The visitors had come about horses, Mr. Mihály Kádár, being the seller, and Mr. Samuel Pelikan, the buyer.

Surely everyone can recognize Mr. Mihály Kádár – a handsome, round-faced man, with his smiling countenance and waxed moustache, and figure curving outwards at the waist. He wore a braided mantle, a round hat, and held a long, thin walking-stick, the top carved to represent a bird's head. His was the group of horses standing beside the pool, with the roan stallion leading them.

Samuel Pelikan was a bony individual, with a large, crooked nose, long beard and moustache, his back and legs somewhat bent from continually trying of horses. There was a crane's feather in his high, wide-brimmed hat, his waistcoat was checked, his jacket short, and his baggy, nankeen trousers tucked into his top-boots. A cigar case was pushed into his side pocket, and he carried a long riding-whip.

These gentlemen, leaving their carriages, walked to the "karám" and shook hands with the overseer, who awaited them there. Then an order was given to the herdsmen, and they all went out to the herd.

Two mounted csikós, with tremendous cracking of whips, rounded up the lot of horses, among which were Mr. Kádár's. There were about two hundred colts in all, some of which had never felt the hand of man. As they drove them in a long curved line before the experts, the horse-dealer pointed out a galloping roan mare to the herdsman on the grass at his side.

"I would like that one!"

Thereupon, Sándor Decsi, casting aside jacket and cloak, seized the coiled-up lasso in his right hand, wound the other end round his left, and stepped towards the advancing herd. Swift as lightning, he flung out the long line at the chosen mare, and with mathematical precision the noose caught its neck instantly, half throttling it. The other colts rushed on neighing; the prisoner remained, tossed its head, kicked, reared, all in vain. There stood the man, holding on to the lasso, as if made of cast-iron, and with his loose sleeves slipping back, he resembled one of those ancient Greek or Roman statues – "the Horse-Tamers." Gradually, in spite of all resistance, and pulling hand over hand, he hauled in the horse. Its eyes protruded, the nostrils were dilated, its breathing came in gasps. Then flinging his arms round its neck, the csikós whispered something in its ear, loosened the noose from its neck, and the wild, frightened animal became straightway as gentle as a lamb, readily resigning its head to the halter. They fastened it directly to the horse-cooper's trap, who hastened to reconcile his victim with a piece of bread and salt.

This athletic display was three times repeated; nor did Sándor Decsi once bungle his work. But it happened the fourth time, that the noose was widely distended, and slipped down to the horse's chest. Not being choked, it did not yield so easily; but commenced kicking and capering, and dragged the csikós, at the other end of the line, quite a considerable distance. But he put forth his strength at last, and led the captive before his owners.

"Truly that is a finer amusement than playing billiards in the 'Bull,'" said Pelikan, turning to Mr. Kádár.

"Well, it's his only work!" returned the worthy civilian.

The horse-dealer, opening his cigar case, offered one to the herdsman. Sándor Decsi took it, struck a match, lit up, and puffed away.

The four raw colts were distributed round the purchaser's carriage; two behind, one beside the near, and the fourth beside the off horse.

"Well, my friend, you're a great, strong fellow!" observed Mr. Pelikan, lighting himself a cigar from Sándor's.

"Yes! If he had not been ill!" grumbled the overseer.

"I wasn't ill!" bragged the herdsman, and tossed back his head contemptuously.

"What on earth, were you then? When a man lies three days in the Mata Hospital –"

"How can a man lie in the Mata Hospital? It is only for horses!"

"What were you doing then?"

"Drunk!" said Sándor Decsi. "As a man has a right to be!"

The old man twisted his moustache, and muttered, half-pleased, half-vexed, "There, you see these 'betyárs'! Not for all the world would they confess anything had ailed them."

Then the time for payment came round.

They settled the price of the four young horses at eight hundred florins.

Mr. Pelikan took from his inner pocket a square folded piece of crocodile leather, this was his purse, and selected a paper from the pile it contained. There was not a single bank-note, only bills, filled in and blank.

"I never carry money about me," said the horse-dealer, "only these. They can steal these if they like, the thieves would only lose by it."

"Which I will accept," said Mr. Kádár in his turn. "Mr. Pelikan's signature is as good as ready-money."

Pelikan had brought writing materials, a portable inkstand in his trouser pocket, and a quill pen in his top-boot.

"We'll soon have a writing-table, too," he remarked, "if you will kindly bring us your horse here, herdsman."

The saddle of Decsi's horse came in very handy as a table on which to fill in the bill. The herdsman watched with the greatest interest.

And not alone the herdsman, but the horses also. Those same wild colts which had been scared four times and from whose midst four of their comrades had just been lassoed, crowded round like inquisitive children, and without the slightest fear. (It is true Mr. Mihály Kádár was bribing them with Debreczin rolls.) One dapple bay actually laid its head on the dealer's shoulder and looked on in wonder. None of them had ever seen a bill filled in before.

It is probable that Sándor Decsi expressed the silent thought of each, when he inquired, "Why do you write 812 florins 18 kreuzers, sir, when the price was settled at eight hundred florins?"

"Well, herdsman, the reason is that I must pay the sum in ready-money. Worthy Mr. Kádár here will write his name on the back, and then the bill will be 'endorsed.' Tomorrow morning he will take it to the Savings Bank, where they will pay out eight hundred florins, but deduct twelve florins – eighteen kreuzers – as discount, and, therefore, I don't require to pay the money for three months."

"And if you do not repay it, sir?"

"Why, then, they will take it out of Mr. Kádár. That is why they give me credit."

"I see. So that is the good of a bill of exchange?"

"Did you never see a bill before?" asked Mr. Pelikan.

Sándor Decsi laughed loud, till his row of fine white teeth flashed.

"A csikós, and a bill!"

"Well, your worthy friend, Mr. Ferko Lacza is quite another gentleman, and he is only a cowherd. He knows what a bill means. I have just such a long paper of his, if you would like to see it."

He searched among his documents, and holding one before the csikós, finally handed him the paper. The bill amounted to ten florins.

"Does Mr. Pelikan know the cowboy?" asked the astonished csikós.

"As far as I know, you do not deal with cattle, sir."

"It is not I, but my wife who has that honor. You see she carries on a little goldsmith business on her own account. I don't meddle in it at all. About two months ago, in comes Mr. Ferko Lacza with a pair of earrings, which he wants gilded, very heavily gilded too!"

Sándor started at that, as if a wasp had stung him.

"Silver earrings?"

"Yes, very pretty silver, filagree earrings, and the gilding came to ten florins. When done, off he went with them – they were certainly not for his own use – and as he had no money he left this bill behind him. On Demeter day he is to meet it."

"This bill?"

Sándor Decsi stared blankly at the paper, and his nostrils quivered. He might have been laughing from the grin on his face, only the writing shook in his two hands. He did not let go of it, but grasped it tightly.

"As the bill appears to please you so well, I will give it you as a tip," said Mr. Pelikan, in a sudden fit of generosity.

"But ten florins, sir, that is a great deal!"

"Of course, it is a great deal for you, and I am no such duffer as to chuck away ten florins every time I buy a horse. But to tell the truth, I should be glad to get rid of the bill under such good auspices, like the shoemaker and his vineyard in the story –"

"Is there something false in it, then?"

"No, nothing false, only too much truth in fact. See, I will explain it to you, please look here. On this line stands 'Mr. Ferencz Lacza,' then comes 'residence,' and after that 'payable in.' Now, in both places 'Debreczin' should be written, but that idiotic wife of mine put 'Hortobágy' instead – which is true enough – for Mr. Ferko Lacza does live on the Hortobágy. Had she written, 'Hortobágy inn' even, I should have known where to find him, but how can I go roaming about the Hortobágy, and the Zám puszta, searching the 'karáms' of goodness knows how many herds, and risking my calves among the watchdogs? I have fought with the woman quite enough about it. Now, at least, I can say I have handed it over at cent. percent interest, and we will have no more rows. So accept it, herdsman. You will know how to get the ten florins out of the cowboy, for you fear neither himself nor his dog."

"Thank you, sir, thank you very, very much."

The csikós folded up the paper and stowed it away in his jacket pocket.

"The young man seems deeply grateful for the ten florin tip," whispered Mr. Kádár to the overseer. "Generosity brings its own reward."

Mr. Mihály Kádár was a great newspaper reader, and took the *Sunday News* and the *Political Messenger*; hence his lofty style of speech.

"That hasn't much to do with his gladness," growled the overseer. "He knows well enough that Ferko Lacza went off to Moravia last Friday; small chance of seeing him or his blessed ten florins again! But he is glad to be clear about the earrings, for there is a girl in that business."

Mr. Kádár raised the bird's-head top of his cane to his lips significantly.

"Aha!" he murmured, "that entirely alters the case!"

"You see the boy's my godson, and I'm fond enough of the cub. No one can manage the herd as he does, and I did my best to free him from soldiering. Ferko is the godchild of my old friend, the cattle overseer, and a good lad also. Both would be the best friends in the world, if the devil, or goodness knows what evil fate, hadn't thrown that pale-faced girl in between them. Now they are ready to eat each other. Luckily my old friend had a capital idea, and has sent Ferko to be head herdsman to a Moravian Duke. So peace will once more reign on the Hortobágy."

Sándor guessed from the whispering that it was of him they were talking, and turned away. Eavesdropping is not congenial to the Hungarian nature. So he drove the herd to the watering-place, where the other horses were already assembled. Five herdsmen there were, three well-poles, one thousand and fifty horses. Each csikós had to lower the pole, fill the bucket, raise the bucket and empty it into the trough, exactly two hundred and ten times. This is their daily amusement, three times repeated, and they certainly cannot complain of lack of exercise!

Sándor Decsi, let no one notice that anything had gone amiss with him. He was merry as a lark, and sang and whistled all day long, till the wide plain resounded with his favorite song:

"Poor and nameless though I be,
  My six black horses I'll drive along.
My six black horses are good to see,
  And the puszta lad is ruddy and strong."

First one, then another csikós caught up the air, filling the whole puszta with their singing. The next day he seemed just as gay, from dawn till dark, as good-humored in fact, "as one who feels himself fey."

After sundown the herds were driven to their night quarters near the "karám," where they would keep together till morning.

Meanwhile the boy brought the bundles of "cserekely," that is, down-trodden reeds, which serve to light the herdsman's fire and to warm up his supper in the kitchen. Very different is the cowherd's meal to that of the csikós. Here is no stolen mutton or pork, such as the csikós of the stage love to talk about. All the swine and flocks pasture on the far side of the Hortobágy river, and it would be a day's journey for the aspiring csikós desirous of bagging a little pig or yearling lamb. Neither is there any of the carrion stew known to and spoken of by the cowboy. The overseer's wife in the town cooks provisions for the herdsmen enough to last a week. As to the fare, any gentleman could sit down to it – sour rye soup, pork stew, "Calvanistic Heaven," or stuffed cabbage, larded meat. All five csikós sup together with the old herdsman, nor is the serving lad forgotten.

A herd of horses differs from a herd of cows after nightfall. Once the cows have been watered, they all settle down in a mass to chew their cud, but the horse is no such philosopher. He feeds on into the night, and as long as there is moon, keeps munching grass incessantly.

Sándor Decsi was in a gay mood that evening, and as they sat round the glowing fire, he asked the overseer, "Dear godfather, how comes it that a horse can eat all day long? If the meadows were covered with cakes, I could never go on stuffing the whole day!"

"Well, godson, I can tell you, only you must not laugh. It is an old tale and belongs to the days when students wore three-cornered hats. I had it from such an inkslinger myself, and may his soul suffer, if every word of it be not true! Once upon a time there was a very famous saint called Martin – he is still about, only nowadays he never comes to the Hortobágy. We know he was a Hungarian saint too, because he always went on horseback. Then there was a King here, and his name was Horse Marot. They called him that because he once managed to cheat Saint Martin of the steed which used to carry him about the world. Saint Martin was his guest, and he tied up his steed in the stable yard. Then one morning early, when Saint Martin wanted to set off on his travels, he said to the King: 'Now give me my horse, and let me start!' 'Impossible,' said the King, 'the horse is just eating.' Saint Martin waited till noon, then he asked for it again. 'You can't go now,' said the King, 'the horse is eating.' Saint Martin waited till sunset, then urged the King once more for his horse. 'I tell you, you can't have your horse, because it's *still eating!'* Then Saint Martin grew angry, cast his little book on the ground, and cursed the King and the horse. 'May the name of 'Horse' stick to you forever! May you never be free of it, but may the two names be said in one breath! As for the horse, may it graze the livelong day yet never be filled!' Since then the horse is always eating, yet never has enough. And you, if you don't believe this story, go to the land of Make-believe, and there on a peak you will find a blind horse. Ask him. He can tell you better maybe, seeing he was there himself."

All the csikós thanked the old man for the pleasant tale. Then each hastened to find his horse, and to trot away through the silent night to his own herd.

Chapter X

It was a lovely spring evening. The sunset glow lingered long in the sky, till night drew on her garment of soft fleecy mists lying all round the horizon.

The sickle of the new moon grazed the Zám Hill, with the lovers' star shining radiant just above – that star which rises so early and sets so soon!

Some distance from the herd, the csikós sought out a resting-place for the night, and there carefully unsaddled his horse and removed the bridle from its head, hanging it on his stick, rammed into the ground. Then he spread the saddle-cloth over the saddle; this was his pillow; his covering the embroidered "szür." But first he broke up some bread, left from his supper, and gave it, in his hand, to the horse.

"Now you may go and graze also, little Vidám (Vidám means gay and lively). You do not feed all day long like the others! You are always saddled, and yet, after you have been ridden the whole day, they want to put you to the machine, and make you draw water. Well, they can want! Do they fancy that 'a horse is as much a dog as a man'?"

Then he gently wiped the horse's eyes with his loose sleeve.

"Now, go and search out good grass for yourself; but don't go far! When the moon has sunk, and with her that shining star, then come back here. See, I don't tether you like a cowherd does, nor shackle your feet as peasants do. 'Tis enough for me to call, 'Here, Vidám!' and you are here directly."

Vidám understood. Why not? Freed from saddle and bridle, he gave a jump, kicked up his hind legs, threw himself on the ground, and rolled over and over several times with his heels to the sky. Then regaining his feet, he shook his mane, neighed once, and started off for the flowery pastures, snorting and flicking his long tail to keep off the humming night insects. The csikós meanwhile lay down on his grassy bed. What a splendid couch! For pillow the wide circle of plain, and for curtains the star-strewn sky!

It was late already. Nevertheless, the earth, like a restless, naughty child, refused to slumber yet. Could not sleep in fact. Everywhere there was sound, soft, indistinct, and full of mystery. The pealing of bells from the town, or the barking of dogs with the cattle were too far away to be heard here. But the bittern boomed among the reeds hard by, like a lost soul, the reed-warbler, the nightingale of the marsh, gurgled and twittered with thousands of frogs to swell the chorus; and through it all came the monotonous clack of the Hortobágy mill. High overhead sounded the mournful wail of flights of wild geese and cranes, flying in long lines, scarcely to be distinguished against the sky. Here and there a dense cloud of gnats whirled into the air, making a ghostly whirring music. Now and then a horse neighed.

Poor lad! formerly your head would hardly touch the saddle before you were fast asleep, now you can only gaze and gaze at the dark blue sky overhead, and the stars, whose names your old godfather taught you. There in the midst is the Pole Star, which never moves from its place; those two are the "Herdsman's Team," while that with the changing color is the "Eye of an Orphan Maid." The brilliant one, just over the horizon, is the "Reaper's Star;" still the "Wanderer's Lamp" is brighter. Those three are the "Three Kings," that cluster the "Seven Sisters," and the star which is sinking into the mist is called the "Window of Heaven."

But why look at the stars when one cannot speak to them? A heavy load weighs down the heart, a cruel wound makes the soul bleed. If one could pour out the bitterness, if one could complain, perhaps it might be easier. But how vast is the puszta and how void!

The shining star set, also the moon. The horse left the pasture and returned to its master. Very gently he stepped along, as if fearing to wake him, and stretching out his long neck, bent his head over him to see if he slept.

"No, I'm not asleep. Come here, old fellow," said the csikós.

At that the horse began to whinny joyously, and lay down near his master.

The herdsman raised himself on his elbows, and rested his head on his hand. Here was someone to speak with – an intelligent beast.

"You see!" he said. "You see, my Vidám? That is the way with a girl! Outside gold, inside silver. When she speaks the truth it is half false; when she lies it is half true! No one will ever learn to understand her. . . . You know how much I loved her. . . ! How often I made your sides bleed as I spurred you on to carry me the quicker to her. . . ! How often I tied you up at the door in snow and mud, in freezing cold and burning sunshine! I never thought of you, my dear old horse, only of how I loved her!"

The horse seemed to laugh at the notion of not remembering. Of course his master had done so.

"And you know how much she loved me. . . ! How she stuck roses behind your ears, plaited your mane with ribbons, and fed you with sweet cakes from her own hand. . . ! How often she drew me back with her kisses, even from the saddle, and hugged your neck that I might remain the longer!"

Vidám answered him with a low whinny. Certainly the girl had done all that.

"Till that confounded beggar slunk in and stole half her heart. If he had but stolen the whole of it! Taken her to himself and gone off with her! But to leave her here; half a heavenly blessing and half a deadly curse –"

The horse evidently wanted to comfort him, and laid his head on his master's knee.

"Strike him, God!" muttered the csikós in an agony of grief. "Do not leave the man unpunished who has plucked another's rose for himself. Did I kill him, I know his mother would weep!"

The horse lashed the ground with his tail, as had his master's rage been transmitted to him.

"But how can I kill him? He is over the hills and far away by now! And you are not able, my poor Vidám, to fly all over the kingdom with me. No, you must stay here with me in my trouble."

Nothing Vidám could do indeed could alter the situation. So he signified his acquiescence in the harsh decree of fate by lying down and stretching out his great head and neck.

But the csikós would not let him turn his thoughts to slumber, he had yet something to tell him. A smacking of the lips, very like a kiss, aroused the horse.

"Don't sleep yet. . . . . I'm not sleeping. We'll have time enough some day when we take our long rest. . . ! Till then we'll keep together we two. . . . . Never shall you leave your master. . . . . Never will he part with you, not though they offer him your weight in gold . . . . my one faithful friend! Do you know how you caught hold of my waistcoat and helped the doctor to lift me up from the ground when I lay on the puszta as good as dead, with the eagles shrieking over me? You seized my clothes with your teeth, and raised me, you did. . . ! Yes. . . ? You know all about it. . . ? my darling! Do not fear, we will never cross the Hortobágy bridge again, never turn in at the Hortobágy inn. . . . I swear it, here, by the starry sky, that never, never, *never* will I step over the threshold where that false girl dwells. . . . May the stars cease to shine on me, if I break my word –"

At this great oath the horse stood up on his fore-feet, and sat like a dog on his hindquarters.

"But don't think we will grow old here," went on the csikós, "we are not going to stick forever on this meadow-land. When I was a little child I saw beautiful tri-color banners waving, and splendid Hussars dashing after them. . . . How I envied them. . . ! Then later, I saw those same Hussars dying and wounded, and the beautiful tri-color flag dragged through the mire, . . . but that will not always last. There will come a day when we will bring out the old flag from under the eaves, and ride after it, brave young lads, to crack the bones of those wicked Cossacks! And you will come with me, my good old horse, at the trumpet's call."

As if he heard the trumpet sounding, Vidám sprang up, pawed the turf with his forefeet, and, with mane bristling and head erect, neighed into the night. Like the outposts of the camp, all the stallions on the puszta neighed back an answer.

"There we'll put an end to this business. . . ! There we'll heal the sorrow and the bitterness, though not by shedding tears! Not the poisoned glass of a faithless maid, nor her more poisonous kisses will destroy this body of mine, but the swordthrust of a worthy foe. Then as I lie on the bloody battlefield, you will be there, standing beside me, and watching over me, till they come to bury me."

And as though to test the fidelity of his horse, the lad pretended to be dead, threw himself limply on the grass, and stretched his arms stark and stiff at his sides.

The horse looked at him for a second, and seeing his master motionless, stepped up with his ears flattened back, and began rubbing his nose against his master's shoulder, then as he did not move, trotted noisily round him. When the clatter of hoofs still failed to waken his master, the horse stood over him, fastened his teeth in the cloak buckled over his shoulders, and began to lift him, till at last the csikós ended the joke by opening his eyes and hugging Vidám with both arms round his neck.

"You are my only true comrade!"

And the horse really laughed! Bared his gums to express his joy, and pranced and capered like any foolish little foal, in his high joy at finding that this dying was only mere fun and pretence. Finally he lay down and stretched himself on the grass. Now *he* was cheating his master and pretending to be dead. Now the herdsman might talk to him and smack his lips all in vain. Vidám would not budge.

So when the csikós laid down his head on the horse's neck, it did very well as a pillow. Vidám raised his head, saw that his master was asleep, and did not make a move till break of dawn.

Even then he would not have stirred, had not his ear been caught by a sudden sound.

Giving a loud snort he woke his master. The csikós jumped from his couch and the horse stood up.

Day was dawning already, and in the east the sky was golden. In the distance the dark form of an approaching horse was visible through the shadowy mist. It was riderless. This is what Vidám had scented.

It was probably a strayed animal, escaped from some herd. For in spring-time, when the fit seizes them, the cowboys' horses, weary of their lonely life among the cattle, and if only they can succeed in breaking their tether, will run, following the scent, to the nearest stud. There a fight takes place, that usually ends badly for the intruders, who are not even shod as are the other horses.

So the runaway would have to be caught.

Hastily bridling his horse, and throwing the saddle on his back, the csikós held the lasso in readiness, and galloped towards the ownerless steed.

But no lasso was needed for its capture! As it neared, it headed of its own accord straight to the csikós, and gave a joyful neigh, to which Vidám responded – these were old acquaintances!

"Now what can this mean?" exclaimed the herdsman, "surely this is very like Ferko's white-faced bay! Yet that must be in Moravia!"

His wonder increased when the two horses meeting, exchanged friendly grunts and began lovingly snuffing each other's chests.

"It is Ferko's horse! There are his initials, 'F.L.,' and for stronger proof, here is actually the scar of the kick it got as a colt!"

The bay had brought the rope along with it, also the peg which it had torn from the ground.

"How come you on the Hortobágy, eh! whiteface?" asked Sándor, while the runaway let him catch it easily enough by the halter still knotted to its head.

"Whence come you? Where is your master?"

But this horse was not in sympathy with him, and did not understand his questions. What can one expect of a horse that spends its life in the company of cattle?

The csikós led his captive to the corral, and there shut it in.

Then he recounted the affair to the overseer.

But as the day advanced, so too did light break on the mystery. From the Zám puszta came the barrow-boy, tearing along in such a hurry that he had even forgotten his cap.

He recognized Sándor Decsi from afar, and made straight for him.

"Morning, Sándor bácsi ('bácsi,' uncle, is a title of respect applied to one's elders. Trans.) Did the bay come here?"

"Yes, indeed. How did it get loose?"

"Had a mad fit. Neighed the whole day. When I tried to groom it, nearly knocked out my eyes with its tail. Then broke loose in the night, and went off with the halter. I've been looking for it ever since."

"And where is its master, then?"

"He's still sleeping – the exertion has quite knocked him up!"

"What exertion?"

"Why, what happened three days back. What, you've not heard of it, Sándor bácsi? How the cows, that the Moravian gentry bought, lost their heads at the Polgár ferry, and slap-bang, bull and all, jumped over the side of the ferry-boat, and tore straight home to the Zám herd. The cowboy could not turn them. He was obliged to come back with them himself."

"So Ferko Lacza is at home again?"

"Yes, but a little more and the overseer would have killed him outright! No, I *never* heard the overseer curse and swear as he did that evening when the herd came rushing over the puszta, Ferko bácsi at their heels. The foam dripped off the horse, and the bull's nose was bleeding. The air was just thick with 'devils,' and 'damns,' and 'gallows trees!' He raised his stick twice to strike the cowboy too, and it swished through the air. 'Tis a marvel he did not beat him."

"And what did Ferko say?"

"Nothing much, only that he couldn't help it, if the beasts chose to go mad.

"'You have bewitched them, you devil!' said the overseer.

"'Why should I do that?' says Ferko bácsi.

"'Why? Because you've been bewitched yourself first. That "Yellow Rose" has given you a charm as she did to Sándor Decsi.'

"Then they began talking about you, Sándor bácsi, but what I could not hear, because they sent me off with a box on the ears, and 'pray what was I listening for? It was none of my business.'"

"So they spoke about me, did they? And about the 'Yellow Rose'?"

"As if I knew or cared about their 'Yellow Rose'! But this I do know, that last Friday when they drove off the cows, Ferko bácsi went into the shanty to fetch his knapsack, and there he pulled out a colored kerchief from his sleeve, and in it a yellow rose was wrapped up. He snuffed at it, and pressed it to his lips till I thought he was going to eat it! Then he unpicked the lining of his cap, pushed in the rose and put it on his head again. Perhaps that was the charm?"

The csikós swinging the loaded end of his cudgel, struck a yellow mullein standing in his path, scattering the blossoms far and wide.

"What harm has the poor 'King's candle' done you?" asked the boy.

But the intent of the blow had been in another direction.

"And now what will happen?" questioned the csikós.

"Well, yesterday, the Moravian drovers turned up on foot, and they discussed the matter with the overseer. So now the cows are to be driven towards Tisza-Füred, and all their calves with them, for over the bridge they surely can't jump! They say the cows ran back to their calves. But Ferko Lacza only laughs to himself."

"And will Ferko Lacza go with them this time?"

"Apparently, since the master never gives him a moment's peace. But the cowboy doesn't want to clear out just yet. He says the cattle must have a day or two breathing time after their race, and he himself sleeps the whole day like a log. Well, 'tis no joke to gallop from Polgár to Zám puszta at one stretch! So the overseer has granted him two days' rest."

"Two days? Two? Surely that is over much."

"I don't know."

"But I do – or else the two days will lengthen into a rest much longer!"

"Well, I must hurry and get the bay home before they are up. Because when the overseer swears at the herdsman, then the cowboy vents all his rage on me. Just wait till I'm herdsman, and then I'll have a barrow-boy of my own to knock about! God bless you, Sándor bácsi."

"He has done that already."

The little lad jumped on the bay, bareback as it was, and stuck his naked feet into its sides. But the bay absolutely refused to stir, turned suddenly right round, and tried to return to the stud. Finally the csikós, taking pity on the boy, brought out his stock-whip, caught it a good thwack in the hind-legs and cracked it two or three times, whereupon the horse, lowering its head, set out full tilt over the puszta, as straight as it could go. The boy had hard enough work to keep his seat, clutching the mane with both hands. The csikós, meanwhile, was quite clear as to his own course.

"Tell Ferko Lacza that Sándor Decsi sends him his respects!" he shouted out after the vanishing "taligás." But whether the boy heard this message is doubtful.

Chapter XI

Next day the csikós went into the "karám," and said to the head herdsman,

"I have some business on hand, godfather, may I take a half-holiday this afternoon? By evening I will be back."

"Certainly you can have leave, my son," replied the old man, "but on one condition. Your are not to enter the Hortobágy inn. Do you understand me?"

"I give you my word of honor not to put a foot inside the Hortobágy inn."

"Very well, I know you will keep your word."

But this, the csikós had omitted to add, "unless I am carried in on a sheet."

It was a hot sultry afternoon when he started, the sky was the color of buttermilk, and the air charged with moisture. The play of the mirage seemed specially fantastic. Not a bird sang overhead, but all sank nestling in the grass. On the other hand the swarms of horse-flies, gad-flies, and midges appeared more wickedly inclined than ever, and the horse could only get along slowly, having to drive off the blood-thirsty torments, now with its hind-foot, now with its head. Still it never missed the path though the bridle lay slack between the csikós' fingers. Man too feels the approach of a storm.

Suddenly, as they reached that substantial triumph of Scythian architecture – the Hortobágy bridge – the csikós started.

"No, no!" he cried. "Here we can't go, old fellow. You know how I swore by the starry heavens never to cross that bridge again."

But never to *ford* the Hortobágy river was not included in his oath.

So he turned down below the mill, and where the water widens into the shallows, waded easily across. The horse had to swim a little, but the herdsman took no heed of that; his fringed linen trousers would soon dry in the hot sunshine.

Then he trotted on to the Hortobágy inn. Here the horse tried to go at a brisker pace, whinnying joyously the while. A glad neigh answered it, for there, tied up to an acacia, stood its comrade – the white-faced bay.

Properly speaking, the Hortobágy inn has no courtyard, for the wide grassy expanse fronting house, stable, and sheds is without fence of any sort. Still it serves as such. A table is put there, and two long benches where the customers sit tippling under the trees.

The csikós sprang from his horse, and tied it up to the other acacia, not that same tree to which the white-faced bay was tethered.

A couple of long-eared steeds were also meditating in the shade of the garden paling, stretching out their necks for the overhanging sprays of barberry, just out of their reach. Their riders were seated at the table, under the acacia, with their fur-lined "bundas" slung over their shoulders, inside out, despite the sweltering weather. In fact, they wore them for shade. As they tippled away, drinking cheap acid stuff out of green glasses, they hummed an endless shepherd's song, monotonous and wearisome. Both were shepherds, whose steed is the donkey.

Sándor Decsi sat down at the further end of the bench, placed his cudgel on the table, and studied the glittering clouds looming heavy on the horizon, and the dark rim of earth beneath. A great yellow pillar rose swirling in one quarter – the whirlwind. Meanwhile the shepherds sang:

"When the shepherd takes his glass,
Sad and mournful grows his ass.
Cheer up, little donkey, grey!
Behind the flock we'll ride away."

This was too much for the csikós to stand.

"See, that's enough, Pista!" he snapped. "For goodness' sake stop that doleful ditty, and get on your grey donkey and trundle after your flock before you're too tipsy to move."

"Dear, dear! Sándor Decsi does seem upset today!"

"I'll upset you worse if you try aggravating me!" said the csikós, and rolled up his shirt sleeves to his elbows. Now he was "ready" for anyone who crossed his path.

The shepherds whispered. Well they knew the puszta rule that when a csikós sits at a table a shepherd may only squat down there with his express permission. If he says, "Get out!" why then the shepherd has to go.

One of them rapped on the table with the bottom of his glass.

"We had better pay, the storm is coming."

The innkeeper's daughter came out at the sound. She made as if she did not see the csikós at all, but attended to the two shepherds, counted up the wine, gave them back the change out of their "dog-tongues," and wiped the table where wine had been spilled. They mounted their donkeys, and being once more in full security, rattled on with their song defiantly:

"Wolves all fear my dogs so strong.
Two lads lead the flock along.
I? Why I ride all the day
On my little donkey grey."

Only when they had quite taken themselves off did the girl address the csikós.

"Well, haven't you even 'good-day' for me, my dearest treasure?"

"Sándor Decsi is my name," growled the herdsman savagely.

"I beg your honor's pardon! Won't you please step into the tap-room, sir?"

"Thanks! I'm well enough out here."

"There you would find fitting society."

"So I see by the horse. He'll come out to me soon enough."

"Well, what can I bring you? Red wine? White wine?"

"No, I won't drink wine," said the csikós. "Bring me bottled beer."

Bottled beer cannot be poisoned. Once the cork is drawn it all froths out.

The girl understood the insinuation. Crushing down the bitterness in her heart she soon returned with a bottle, which she placed before the lad.

"What is this?" he cried. "Am I a cobbler's apprentice, to have *one* bottle brought me?"

"Very well, sir. Please don't be angry. I'll bring more directly."

This time she came back with a whole bundle, and set all six in a row before him.

"That is better," said he.

"Shall I draw the cork?"

"Thanks! I can do it myself."

He took the first bottle, broke off the neck against the edge of the table, and poured the foaming beer into the tall glass beside him. It costs more like this, because the broken bottle has to be paid for; but then, "a gentleman is always the gentleman."

The girl moved off airily, shaking her sides flippantly as she went. Her golden earrings tinkled. Her hair was down again, no longer twisted round the comb, and the ribbon ends fluttered coquettishly behind her. "As thou to me. So I to thee."

The csikós sat quietly drinking his beer, and the girl sang on the verandah:

"Hadst thou known what I know,
Or whose sweetheart am I!
Not alone would I weep,
Thou wouldst cry."

At the fourth line the door was shut with a bang.

By the time she reappeared again, three empty broken-necked bottles stood on the table. Klári took them, picking up the broken bits of glass into her apron.

After the third bottle, the lad's humor had changed, and as the girl fussed round him, he suddenly slipped his arm round her waist.

She made no demur on her part.

"Well, may one call you 'Sándor' again?" she asked.

"You always could. What did you want to say?"

"Did you ask anything?"

"Why are your eyes so red?"

"Because I am so happy. I have a suitor."

"Who?"

"The old innkeeper at Vervölgy. He is a widower with lots of money."

"Shall you accept him?"

"Why not, if they take me to him? Let me go!"

"*You lie, lie!* You cover up your lying, and so lie worse than ever!" cried the lad.

He removed his hand from the girl's waist.

"Will you drink more?" she asked.

"Why not?"

"But you'll get fuddled from so much beer."

"Much need of it too to quench the fire burning in me. See you give the one in there plenty of strong wine. Heat him up with it, so that we may match each other."

But she took good care not to tell "the one inside" "about the other" out here.

The csikós took the matter into his own hands. He began to sing, selecting the mocking air with which they are wont to tease the cowherds:

"Oh I am the Petri cowboy bold,
I guard the herd on the Petri wold.
My comrades can go
Through the mire and snow;
I lie on my feather-bed safe from cold."

Well thought! Hardly was the verse at an end before out came his man. In one hand he carried his bottle of red wine, with the tumbler turned over the top, in the other his cudgel. Setting down his wine opposite the csikós, he next laid his cudgel beside the other one, and then took his seat at the table exactly facing the other lad.

They neither shook hands nor spoke a word of greeting. Each gave a silent nod, like two between whom speech is unnecessary.

"So you are back from your journey, comrade?" asked the csikós.

"I'll be off again directly if I have the mind."

"To Moravia?"

"Yes, if I don't change my plans."

They both drank. After a pause the csikós began again.

"Are you taking a wife with you this time?"

"Where should I get a wife?"

"I'll tell you. —— take your own mother!"

"She wouldn't give up being a Debreczin market-woman for the whole of Moravia!"

They both drank again.

"Well, have you bidden your mother farewell?" asked the csikós.

"I have bidden her farewell."

"And squared all your accounts with the overseer?"

"Certainly."

"You owe *nobody* anything?"

"What extraordinary questions you do ask to be sure!" exclaimed the cowboy.

"No, I am not in debt, even to the priest. What does it matter to you?"

The csikós shook his head, and broke the neck of another bottle. He wished to fill his friend's glass, but the cowboy placed his hand over it.

"You won't drink my beer?"

"I'm keeping to the rule. Wine on beer – never fear. Beer on wine – no time."

The csikós poured himself out the whole bottle, and then began to moralise (the not unfrequent result of beer-drinking).

"See, comrade," he said, "there is no uglier sin in the world than lying. I once lied myself, though not in my own defense, and it has oppressed my soul ever since. Lying does well enough for shepherds, but not for lads on horseback. The first shepherd of all was a liar. Jacob, the patriarch, lied when he deceived his own father, making his hands rough like Esau's. So little wonder if his followers, who keep flocks, should live by lies. It may suit a shepherd, but it is not for a cowboy."

The cowherd went into roars of laughter.

"I say, Sándor, what a good parson you would make! You can preach as well as the Whit-Sunday probationer at Balmaz Újváros."

"Yes? Well, comrade, maybe you would not mind my turning out a good preacher, but if I turned out a good lawyer, you might care more. So you say you don't owe a crooked kreuzer to any human being?"

"Not to any human soul."

"Without lying?"

"No need for it."

"Then what is this? This long paper? Do you recognize it?"

The csikós pulled out the bill from his pocket, and held it before his companion's nose.

The cowboy turned suddenly crimson with anger and shame.

"How did that come into your hands?" he demanded angrily, and springing from his seat.

"Honestly enough. Sit down, comrade," said the csikós. "I am not asking any questions, only preaching. The good man who got this bill instead of money came to our place not long ago to buy horses. He paid with a bill of exchange, and when I asked what it meant, explained, mentioned that you knew the use of a bill, and then showed me your writing, complaining bitterly that there was some omission, that it was only made payable on the Hortobágy, and that the Hortobágy is a wide word. So now I have brought you the bill for you to correct the mistake. Don't let a horse-cooper say that a Hortobágy cowboy cheated him! Fill in the line, 'Payable on the Hortobágy, in the inn courtyard.'"

The csikós spoke so mildly that he entirely misled his companion. He began to think that after all nothing was called into question here but the honor of csikós and cowboys.

"All right, I will do as you wish," he said.

They rapped on the table, and Klárika came out (she had been lurking near the door). Great was her surprise when, instead of witnessing a bloody encounter, she beheld the two young men conferring peaceably together.

"Fetch us pen and ink, Klári, dear," they said.

So she brought writing materials from the town commissioner's room. Then she looked on to see what would be done.

The csikós showed the paper to the cowherd, pointing with his finger where, and dictating what to write.

"'Payable on the Hortobágy,' so much is written already, now add, 'in the inn courtyard.'"

"Why in the *courtyard?*" inquired the cowboy.

"Because – because it can't be otherwise."

Meanwhile the storm was nearing rapidly. A hot wind preceded the tempest, covering earth and sky with yellowish clouds of dust. Birds of prey hovered shrieking over the Hortobágy, while flocks of swallows and sparrows hurried under the shelter of the eaves. A loud roar swept over the puszta.

"Won't you come indoors?" urged the girl.

"No, no, we can't," answered the csikós, "our work is out here."

When the cowherd had finished writing, then the csikós took the pen from his hand, and turning over the bill, inscribed his name on the back, in big roundhand characters.

"Now, what is the sense of you writing your name there?" asked the cowboy, inquisitively.

"The use is, that when the pay-day comes round, then *I* and *not you* will pay those ten florins."

"Why should you, instead of me?"

"Because it is *my debt!*" said the csikós, and clapped his cap to his head. His eyes flashed.

The cowboy paled all at once. Now he knew what awaited him. The girl had learnt nothing from the scribbling nor from the discourse. She shook her head. "They were very foolish," she thought, and the gilded earrings tinkled in her ears. "'This,' and 'that,' and 'Yellow Rose,' they must be talking about her!"

But the csikós carefully folded the paper, and handed it to her. Very gently he spoke,

"Dear Klári," he said, "please be so very kind and put this safely away in your drawer. Then should Mr. Pelikan, the horse-dealer, come in here to dine on his way back from Onod fair, give it him. Tell him that we sent it, we two old comrades, Ferko Lacza, and Sanyi Decsi, with our best respects. One of us will meet it, which, time will show."

The girl shrugged her shoulders. "Funny people! Not a thought of quarreling in their heads! Signing their names to the same paper."

She collected the writing materials and carried them back to the commissioner's room, at the end of the long pillared verandah. The two lads were left alone together.

Chapter XII

The csikós quietly emptied his last bottle of beer. The cowboy poured out the rest of his red wine into the glass.

They clinked glasses.

"Your health!" It was drained at a breath.

Then the csikós began. Leaning on his elbows he remarked,

"This is a fine large puszta, this Hortobágy, eh, comrade?"

"Truly it is!"

"I hardly think the desert could have been larger where Moses kept the Jewish people wandering for forty years!"

"You must know best, you are always poring over the Bible!"

"Still, though the Hortobágy be so large, there is not room enough on it for both you and me."

"I say the same."

"Then let us rid it of one of us!"

With that they caught up their cudgels, two oak saplings from the Csát forest, the club end heavily loaded.

Each went to his horse. Cowboys do not fight on foot. When the girl returned from the house, both were in the saddle.

After that no word was spoken. Silently turning their backs on each other, one went right, one left, as if flying before the approaching storm. When there was about two hundred paces between them, they glanced back simultaneously, and turned their horses. Then swinging their cudgels, both lads put spurs in their horses, and rushed at each other.

This is the duel of the puszta.

It is not as easy as it looks. Fighting with swords on horseback is an art, but the sword where it strikes inflicts a wound not easily forgotten. He who wields the cudgel must aim his blow for the one instant when his galloping steed meets his opponent's. There is no parrying possible, no thrusting aside of the stroke. Who strikes truest wins the day.

The two herdsmen, meeting at the cudgel's length, struck at each other's head, then dashed past on their horses.

Sándor Decsi shook in the saddle, his head fell forward from the force of the blow, but tossing it back directly, he straightened his crumpled cap. Evidently his crown had only felt the handle of the cudgel.

His stroke had been better aimed. The loaded end hit his adversary's skull, who, turning sideways, tumbled out of the saddle, and fell face downwards on the ground. The victor bringing up his horse, thereupon promptly cudgelled his fallen foe from the crown of his head to the sole of his foot, nor spared a square inch of him. For such is the custom.

If gentlemen of higher rank would only adopt it, God knows how rare duels would become!

Having ended this business, the csikós picked up his opponent's cap on the point of his stick, tore out the lining, and found beneath a withered yellow rose. He threw it up in the air, giving it a knock which sent the petals flying in a hundred pieces, and floating like butterflies down the wind.

"I told you beforehand, didn't I?" shouted the csikós from on horseback to the girl, who had watched this decisive combat from the inn door. He pointed to his mangled opponent. "There! Take him in and nurse him! You may have him *now!*" A hissing thunderbolt fell before the mill close by. Here was the storm. All round them the sky crashed and crackled.

"You see," said the girl, "had he struck you instead, I would have thrown my own body over you, and protected you from his blows! Then you would have known how truly I loved you!"

The csikós put spurs to his horse, and galloped off into the storm. Sheets of rain and hail fell in torrents, thunder crashed with a blinding flash. The girl gazed after the horseman till the storm hid him from view. Once or twice when it lightened his figure shone visible through the fiery rain, then she lost sight of it, till at last it vanished utterly.

Perhaps she never saw him again.

Lightning Source UK Ltd.
Milton Keynes UK
UKOW050649060213

205902UK00001B/89/P